Rising Depth
phase 01 of The Renpet Phenomenon

DjaDja N Medjay

Copyright 2020 by DjaDja N Medjay

Edited by Valjeanne Jeffers

Cover Art by Cassandra Mark

all rights reserved. No part of this book may be reproduced in any manner whatsoever without written permission from the author.

Contact the author at: th3rp1@gmail.com

and therenpetphenom.com

Printed in the United States of America.

Be a self-sustaining sun amongst harmonious stars

Rising Depth

Chapter 1

6:00am

Shiiitt … it's freezing under her bed.

Keeping my body crunched up in a ball, tensing up for heat, without making any noise isn't easy against her cold ass floor. I can't remember too many times something like this happened to me … needing to be quiet and still underneath a mattress. The last few years, not counting the times spent in those cramped and poorly lit shelters during RP Events, it was me always on the move, never stopping for rest.

And for what?

All that crap only amounts to four years of SUNY turnt up walking around the campus in a fog, landing a no-where job at Directive Living after graduation …

And me being stuck under here.

There's nothing in front of my eyes, but the darkness of night staring right back at me. Luckily, since there is nothing to see, I won't get all dizzy. The throbbing in my head is an almost tolerable running off the mouth friend. The sake' and shoju won't come down off my breath tho'. The stink keeps running back into my nose every time I try to gently breath out my mouth.

How long do I have to be sandwiched up between the Hell of the floor and the weight coming down on me of what was supposed to be my Heaven? I really thought she was mine…How could she do this to me?

Heaven and Hell? Neither are really my beliefs, so why even think about it like that? Instead, I think about the thirty minutes of over a hundred places on my skin irritating the mess of out of me, just pushing me to give myself away by scratching. Ignoring it only makes it worse, even itchier each time the morning's cold drafts of air run over my body. I'm gonna get a cold if this keeps up.

Hate the winter, even more the POS landlords for turning the heat off after 1am. Bastards … Damn! I just want to be able to moooove, at least my shoulders or something.

At this point, whether it's pins and needles, or just plain old itchy skin, it's too hard to tell. Especially as a man who's been through all sorts of shit in college, and even more on the streets. Some tight situations left scars on my body, the rest somewhere in my head.

Not all of them healed and only a few were resolved. But one thing I could never bear was a stubborn old itch. *That* was the worst thing someone could sit through.

Even squirming just enough for my skin to rub against this coarse ass rug isn't doing anything for me. *Can't keep taking these drafts. Please, please don't let me sneeze.*

Wait a minute, they stopped talking! What's going on up there?

This is so humiliating. What the kind of stand-up dude would let this happen to them? Fuuuuck!

There was no one to turn to for help or comfort either. *Thanks Mom and Dad. Yeah, appreciated the upbringing. Or the lack of it.* Other people get to lean on a God up in the sky somewhere, to the point that they can gain some solace.

But not me. oh no.

Being raised in the Kemetic System without being allowed to lean on the Netcheru or even the ancestors for tight situations…*I got myself into*…always sucked. Mom and Dad made sure no God Concept or God Complex ever entered my train of thought. Which made it easier for other things to enter.

A whole lot of things.

Man up! Stop acting like a little bitch right now.

"*Uhh.*" The moan comes through the mattress—as if her lips are pressed against my ear.

At least, it helps me to keep everything in perspective; otherwise, this whole thing would be one long psychotic episode. Really, more moaning? Into groaning? It keeps vibrating pass the mattress and against my back—literally rubbing it in.

But *he is rubbing it* in the lady I thought was mine.

This can't be happening. Achy … and so sleepy. I want to yawn so bad, so tired …

7:00am

Huh?

Wow, glad that didn't spill out my mouth when my eyes flicked opened. Asleep … fell asleep. What the hell? Who does that in this type of situation?

Damn.

Everything is numb. Well, it feels that way from the neck down. I can't even move to shake my legs out a little.

At least the worn lace of the dust skirt allows me to see the faint beams of the early sun dragging across the floor. I'm getting all mesmerized by the specks of dust flitting about in its light.

It's morning! Something has got to give—and soon. It must be getting close to 7am, need to be getting to work soon.

<<YOU HAVE ONE HOUR BEFORE THE 8AM EXPRESS>>

Between the popping and stabs of treble scraping against my eardrums, the cyber-trans from my **I-plant** struggles with its garbage 6G tech to be clear.

Sigh. Look at all this shit around me.

You never know what lies under a person's bed until forced underneath it—especially when one side of your face is pressed up against a rug that feels like it's never been get vacuumed.

To make matters worse, there's the stench that's crept into my nose for the past hour or so. At first, the slight scent of food was nothing to be bothered with; just what was there. But the grittiness from the rug has had time to get further into my skin, with my nose just sitting there figuring out different smells—smells that are rotting, turning my stomach even further.

It stinks—want to throw-up. Shiiit … moved the wrong way.

Muscles cramped up in my lower back like something had bit into it. All this is becoming too much.

Uh…okay, it's slowly letting go. Are those scattered fast-food wrappers around me? Eatys Shack, Donut Hut, King's Chicken—her diet is horrible. No wonder she menstruates for so long.

Some wrappers, even in the lack of light, looked like they had pieces of food stuck in them. Come to think of it, I could feel some bits of food mashed into tufts of the rug.

For real tho', you must be kidding me? How come I didn't see this before about her? Does she eat on the bed and toss garbage under it?

There's a trash-can right next to the dresser, WTF?

"Get on your knees and poke that ass out," growled the dude that I was abruptly told about in the not too distant past, his voice all heated and heavy.

Loose screws and bolts in the bedframe sound like the Up-Metro express hitting a bad stretch of track. *Is that the post slamming into the wall, is that sheetrock breaking and tumbling down inside of it?*

Fuuccck! My back again. Gotta chill, relax…let it go.

Me and this chick is done.

I'm feeling all sorts of nasty. I want to scrub the mess out of my tongue and nut-sack. All the heavy pounding and smacking of flesh on flesh is muffled by the mattress, but still loud enough to take stabs at my chest. This dude must be tall and heavy, got me ducking areas of the bed sinking in all over the place…like a game of Whack a Mole.

"Oh, Oh, Oh, yes, *yes!* Harder! *Harder!*"

She never made those soft pants for me, they just pouring effortlessly out her mouth for this dude.

She gave me none of that enthusiasm.

I sigh—but not too loud. I'm gonna try to move around a bit, get some blood pumping into these numbed-up arms and legs that didn't seem attached to me anymore. Just in case this ef'd up situation leads me to having to thump. I want to be ready.

Maybe I can stretch out too, literally under their humping, and get my fingers to my neck. Glad my nails don't get trimmed down all that much, cause they and my fingers are scratching all these itches to death. Need to force myself off my neck like a PCD Depressant addict on the verge of OD.

Wait, my fingers feel wet. I didn't scratch hard enough to break the skin, so I can't be bleeding ... something pulpy is sliding between them. Great, my cell is still charged and on *... Okay, it's on silent, get the LCD light to see.*

Now, let's see what's on my hand ...

A roach.

Seeing parts of it mangled and strewn across my fingers doesn't bother me much; in fact, it doesn't faze me at all. Simply wipe it off across a patch of rug away from my face.

What gets me though was that all this time I thought my skin was itchy, there were bugs crawling all over me. The cell's flashlight has not just one or two, but a bunch of these mofos scampering about as the light hits them.

And *that* wouldn't be such a big deal if I weren't completely *naked*. Earlier, when the front door magna-lock clicked open, the words "Hurry that's my boyfriend coming home from the correctional facility!" escaped frantically from her mouth and slammed around my head.

Which only left me seconds to grab my clothes and slip under her bed, despite the sudden head-rush that struck me like a punch to the nose. He practically galloped down the hallway, beating into the old wooden floor with horse hooves.

Whew! I just made it under the bed in time—to see his big ass feet and the tattered bottoms of his blue workpants head over to the bed.

And that was hours ago.

"I can't believe I was *right* all this time. I got something for your lying ass." he muttered. His soft voice doesn't hide the intensity of his words.

It's unreal.

"I knew someone was here ... Or still *is* here." I can hear the anger boil underneath his breath.

"No one's here, Wayne! You *know*—!"

The smack that struck *her* jolted *me*. I didn't have to see it to know how hard he brought his hand down on her face. I heard it. I wish these chills would stop running up and down my back so I can think.

He did that to her.

What was this guy gonna do if he finds out there *is* someone under *his* bed? I can't stop the scenarios flashing before my eyes. No man wants to find another man in their bedroom, especially one that's naked.

Shit! What am I going to do?

He hit her again, harder.

Toni ...

The legs of the bed won't stop hopping up and down from off the floor. She must be struggling against him.

"No, *no!* I don't know what you're talking about!" Her voice was strained, weakly choking out the words. *"Please stop hitting me! You're home now … You're home!"* she begs.

It's all fucked up. Her tone, although stressed, carries no strong distress. This has happened before. *This was probably why she would start phone arguments with me, so I wouldn't be able to see her. So, she could heal from this asshole beating her.*

He more than likely beats her until he feels some sort of control, control that he does not have in his own life. Or over himself.

There are times that me being able to quickly assess these things just sucks.

"I see." He doesn't sound human anymore. "No real man would stay quiet when a woman was getting beat." These words were without emotion—followed by blows.

His words were a fucked-up contradiction, and he knew it. A part of me, long dead, is coming back to life. A familiar, buried urge running around in my chest…into my hands.

Rage.

What the…? The weight of the bed is shifting above me, Toni's body flies across the room slamming roughly into the dresser—slumping up against it. Her entire naked body trembles down to her feet, then slowly goes limp.

I can barely move. My muscles ache from dragging myself closer to the foot of the bed. I can't stand the sight of her chin falling to her chest …

What I see of her face is almost unrecognizable.

Going to get my pants on, whether he hears me or not. Oh shit, he's running over to her!

"NOOOOOOO!" His howling bellowed into my ears. "I didn't *mean* it! *I didn't mean it, Toni!*" The bastard has the nerve to hold her smashed and bleeding face in his hands, looking into her eyes.

Collapsing by her side, drool shakes wildly from his quivering bottom lip. The mofo just sits there blubbering on and on while hitting the floor with his fists, gradually falling on his side. I'm starting to feel like I can get at this dude— run up and bash his head against something while he lies crumpled over there. The only thing keeping him from seeing me is his grief and this beat-up bed skirt…

And my pussiness.

He gets up too abrupt for his body to handle, and almost crashes into the dresser himself before scrambling about the room, knocking shit over in the process.

Why did he stop moving? Why is he staring at the ceiling, like something is there? He's going crazy, swatting at the air, and trying to grab onto something in front of him … that's not there.

"Leave me alone! LEAVE ME ALONE!" I never heard a man scream out like that before.

It serves him right to go crazy. Well, he's not that far gone; he still has some sense, seeing as he stopped with the outbursts and got his clothes on.

He keeps pausing then goes back to stuffing random things into his duffle bag. Now, he's using the cloth he grabbed from out one of the drawers to wipe down the handle. His focus is all over the place, wiping off random areas the room.

Why did he stop to look at Toni?

The sick bastard crouches down next to her and starts to gently wipe the blood off her face, causing it to only bleed more.

Now what you going to do with the cloth smart-ass?

It's like he heard me, the way he just stumbles into the bathroom and begins flushing again and again.

"Fuck it. It finally went down." I can hear his voice echoing out with the last flush.

Now he's back in here again. The asshole keeps looking around the room— like he didn't make a thorough check of everything before. As he speeds out the room ...

Caught a look at his face!

The front door slammed, and the magna-lock clicks. *It's safe to come out. He's not coming back. Fuuuuccck.*

Everything in my head and chest suddenly gets heavy and shit, fighting against me moving. It's becoming more than a struggle to drag myself out from my hiding place, each time I pull myself forward, my arms ache, then go dead. I really want the things in the rug brought in from the street to stop scraping against my body.

Okay…out from underneath the bed. Now what?

I can barely feel my legs, so I crawl over to Toni. I can't stop breathing hard, my freakin' chest is closing, wanting to explode. Straining to inhale keeps giving me a full whiff of her scent still on me.

Mouth going dry … throat doing the same.

But I still haul myself over to her, pulling along the deadweight in my limbs. Cold air keeps driving itself against my naked body, almost as if it senses I'm the only source of heat in the room. The chill, that had just about frozen my spine, seems to be reaching out from my back for the building drafts around me. And the sun is being really shitty right now, with its light shining through the window and blanketing her face.

It's more than unrecognizable. It's *broken*.

The life that filled it earlier when we made love is *gone*. Wiped away. And her exposed body doesn't move an inch, nor does her chest rise and fall.

She's dead.

No…wait! There's warmth coming from her!

"… trrr …" softly leaves her lips.

"Toni …*Toni!*" *She must be still alive. Please, please don't let this be her last breath.*

But it is. Only cold … deep cold between us now.

I want to reach out and touch her— let her know someone cared— but I gotta fight the feeling before my hand touches her face. This place became a murder scene real quick, and I need to get up out of here.

C'mon, bruh, force control back from the stiffness in your legs, even with all this grogginess rolling around in your head.

My instincts keep me scanning around the room. It only makes me feel worse with what is seen and *seen into*. All the girly things, pink fluffy pillows and stuffed dolls stand out, reminding me of her warm spirit. I can't help melting into the eyes of Mr. Daniels, that large stuffed animal I won for her at a company fair, sitting up in the corner there, worn, and dirty.

Sigh.

This is too freakin' surreal. I can't tell if it's my emotions, or if actual things around the room are *touching me*. The stank of sex getting all up into my nose, and the feeling, the feeling of having it still heavy in the air, running right along with that stale and grim cold draft.

I can't think straight, heart's pounding like it wants to burst through my chest. I keep tripping over her legs, trying to get the rest of my clothes on, her cold skin slipping against mine.

Shit! My prints—my signature— are all over her.

This wooziness taking my head for a spin and the idea of jail doesn't sit well with me. It's too difficult to keep standing.

I can't stand anymore, so why try to? Damn my knees banged against the floor harder than I thought they would. But forget about that now, I gotta get something to wipe my signatures off Toni. The pant leg of my jeans that should be enough to rub them out of her leg—that's where my foot made contact, right?

What am I doing?

The denim is heating up, starting to burn into her skin, and me hunching over this way keeps pulling at my lower-back.

<<YOUR CORTISOL AND ADRENALINE LEVELS ARE RISING – DO YOU NEED ASSISTANCE?>>

Shit, I need to watch it!

That newly required **EMO-SENSOR** app from **I-plant,** forced upon me at work, may alert some type of authorities to arrive here. I don't need that. It's getting brighter in here with more light breaking through the window.

Getting late.

I got to stop, stop rubbing against her leg like I'm trying to get a stain out of my clothes. Shock is interfering with my cognition, it still has me treating her body as if it were stained cloth, not another human being.

Okay, stopping. Not doing it anymore. Not doing it anymore. My fingers are cramping up. I need to get out of here—now! *Arrrgh. Rug burn.*

Why was diving back underneath the bed for my boots, coat and shirt, a good idea?

'Cause you scared bitch.

All mixed-up in my head, and with the pain growing, swirling in my chest is making it too hard to find a way to calm down. Every breath is a fight against the empty feeling building in my heart. I barely got enough strength to get my arms down the sleeves of my coat.

Stop sweeping the room with your eyes, you got everything, head for the open window. Still shaking ... c'mon, just breathe and relax get the sleeves of the coat over your hands and grab for the bottom of the window.

Crap, it's all out the grooves. I guess this is how thieves do it, keeping your cool under the pressure of being seen by nosey ass neighbors.

Can't stop my head from swinging back to look at Toni.

This was my fault...

Damn! This winter wind blowing in and smothering my face, instantly wakes me up from the daze I'm falling back into.

Sigh. Need to get down this raggedy looking ass fire-escape. Why every fire-escape rung hit by my feet feels like it's about to drop off? And all the clanging got me hiding my face.

Dashing past these apartment windows anyone can see me. Luckily, this rusted piece of shit is in the back of the building and she was only on the third floor.

Was…

Finally, in the alley, must get on to the street. Don't run, blend evenly with the pace of the crowd. Act normal and keep a cool head, them **EMO-SENSORS,** on each street post, detect changes in neural and hormonal activity. Police were soon to follow when your emotional state bordered on what they thought was threatening to the city … or more so the property. I need to stop thinking about any DNA left around unwittingly. I did use a condom. But shit, I was butt ass naked under that bed for a while … what about that?

And it just hit me, my entire body was on hers.

This is not right. Have I grown this cold? Let me get this half-finished pint of Babacut Rum out my pocket and get a taste, ahhh … got some fire back in my legs and warmth in my chest.

What about the murder I just witnessed?

What About the confused young lady who lost the tortured life she must have led? What about what little bit of love that I had growing for her? *My Muwt would say I am undoing all the years of cultural fortitude her and Baba instilled in me with all of this.*

Why am I so rebellious to my true self?

I'm shuffling mindlessly past these people in the busy morning streets and the smells of electrical pulsing flying overhead … and directly in front of me, has me feel lost and *alone* in all of it. And even though I think I am unnoticed, it's like the eyes of everyone passing me by see more than my face. Eyes cutting into me along with this bitter wintry air. Like they can read all that went on back at the apartment and see my cowardice. And their faces may be saying one thing, but they too could be like Wayne: a powder keg ready to blow. Or they could be ready to snitch to the Novus City Police Authorities in exchange for free upgrades and medical services.

I want to believe this to be untrue, I really do. But as Baba would say, *"Belief only makes electrons stagnate…where Knowing gets them to flow."*

Why these chilling gusts of wind keep striking at my face? Pulling away from my skin while the agonizing idea of having to ride the train fills my head.

<WEEEOOONG> <WEEOOONG>

<ATTENTION. UNSCHEDULED RP ACTIVITY WILL HIT THIS SECTOR IN APPROXIMATELY 2 MINUTES>

This woman walking close to me is getting aggressive — pushing me aside—followed by some street-kid. Like a domino effect, droves of folk sway into different groups. Everyone who's on the street drops their shit and scatters during the warning, echoing out a lifeless mechanical chant, before it fades out over building rooftops.

The group I'm in is swept along with it, against my will, steadily piling into a nearby shelter—bumping reluctantly against each other … *and letting any beef go.*

Already jammed into this shelter's compact space as it is, the special chemically treated reinforced UV resistant door keeps forcing us in further, sealing shut behind us. Okay, can stop looking folks in the face, it's easy to see there's ten of us in here.

At least we won't be cold with all this body heat in such a tight space, especially from us Nubians.

<STANDBY>   <STANDBY>   <STANDBY>

"Could you suck your chest in a bit more? Damn!" snapped the well-endowed mocha-toned woman I'm mashing up against, apparently irritated by her breasts rolling across my chest.

Common sense would tell her that my chest can't go in any further than it already is—wait a minute, what does that faded, and partially shredded Inspector Tag plastered against the wall say? "Shelter Inspection Rating D – Insufficient RP Shielding."

Um … that can't be good.

"Let me in! *Let me in!*"

Some Euro, from what I could make out through the small dingy portal window, started banging like crazy against the metal slab of a door, begging to be let in. We all just watch him, unable to do anything *but* watch. *When* it was over *then* the sensors would release the door.

<<INCOMING CALL FROM MUWT>>

Shit! Why does she always call me at the worst time?

Oh c'mon, the constant dull ringtone beep won't go away. I can't reach for my cell or focus well enough to neuro-reject the call. … but picking up is easily triggered simply by swallowing. *What's with these program designers?*

"Hey Ma, can't talk right now." that came out meekly, but still managed to piss off everyone around me for having a low grade I-plant plan.

"Is my baby okay? I heard that the CME forecasted a week ago would arrive today. Are you safe?" She blurted out almost loud enough for everyone to hear—and nearly bursting my head from her voice going off like a megaphone. "And stop calling me Ma … its *Muwt*…and another thing—!"

"Ma! I mean Muwt—!"

Without warning the call drops, and the cold screeching of feedback stabs at my eardrums.

\<RP EVENT NOW\>
\<STAY CLEAR OF THE WINDOW\>

Arrghh! The blast of light flushing through the portal, nearly blinds all of us. Even with its own shielding. That's right, today wouldn't be just a string of low-level RP Events. Novus City was going to get hit hard with a CME, not just a few solar flares.

It's here.

There goes that red light, those of us who been in RP Event Shelters know it all too well, flicking on above us, which seems to click on just when a CME strikes. By the looks on people's faces, everyone, including myself, were disturbed and made uneasy by the Euro still screaming his head off outside of the shelter's door. But, little by little, his pounding is growing faint. The light continues to pour in through the portal as his hollow thumps become slower ... lighter.

It's over.

Tightly bundled in this shelter, our chests pressed up against one another before letting out one unified gasp—followed by silent stares. Just when my next breath forgot about the lady and fully expanded my chest, the flickering red emergency light shut off. The door is having some trouble sliding open, eerily scraping against the runners, the sharp squeaking sound makes my stomach cramp. Finally, fully open, a gust of air carrying the smell of burned flesh fills the shelter. People's eyes tear up as they fumble to block their noses. The tit-lady takes three steps out the shelter, then heaves over and vomits.

Me ... I'm just watching everyone else. Stuck. Not really feeling much.

Damn. I should have stayed in the shelter longer; it's hard to breathe, much less walk through this microwave of heat. WTF? What am I tripping over…? Oh shit!

The Euro. His body is smoldering but becoming visible as the smoke about him rises and breaks up. His hands, what's left of them, clutch at an unopened tube of Melanocyl X. Most of his face is hidden by the steamy vapors coming off it, except the sunlight reflecting off his jaw— the bone stripped clean and gleaming.

<RP EVENT OVER>

<PLEASE MAKE A SCHEDULED THERAPY APPOINTMENT IF NEEDED AT YOUR LOCAL DL AUXILLARY UNIT>

Chapter 2

8:15am

With each gentle rock of the train, my eyelids want to fall completely shut, and I'm getting tired of stopping them. Nothing is in this train car with me except the sounds of grinding track, the plexi-glass damn near shaking out of the frames and the occasional deafening screech.

But every time the lights went completely out, and the car was near pitch black, I could have sworn there were strange things moving about in the shadows.

Or maybe my mind is playing tricks on me.

Keep dozing off though, for how long and between which stops only the train car knew … Huh? Whuu-ut? Shit … drifted again.

It sucks to wake up, just to continue in and out of sleep, jerking and banging my head against the subway map behind me.

And that's the least of my worries.

Every moment, just before I pass out, Toni's lifeless face pops up in front of me—her beautiful caramel-skin devoid of life.

It's nearby.

The thing, the noise, the *whatever*, that made me stop wanting to take the train. Why are my senses locking into all the sensations from when it happened a few months back?

That's why I stopped riding the train.

The day it happened was no different from my other days riding Novus City's knock-off of the original Hyperloop. The train was packed wall to wall, filled with useless conversations and a thousand different body odors…like any other day.

Then it struck me.

The high-pitched noise that came without warning. It didn't seem to mess with anyone else around me. *Only me. I really need to tell my parents about it. They would know what to do.*

It was the first time I threw up on the train and the first time I saw how a crowd of people could give less of a shit about you. Then there were all those weeks after that … an excruciating siren-like blast would stab at the inside of my ears when I was between certain stations. Especially when the train passed through the midsection of *The Bridge.*

That's when riding the train became impossible for me…so I started to bike and carpool to work through the Up-Metro Express Extension and its own dangers. Internet searches only led me to ghost stories in Japan (more than I cared to sit through on YouTube) and over a thousand references in Nubian Culture referring to the

Afterlife and Underworld. Nothing I found triggered an acceptance or even some type of comfort.

Didn't expect to be re-capping that whole experience again.

And now, the swaying of the train that once brought me peace of mind seems to be bent on taunting me with its earsplitting sounds. Getting close to one of those places in the tunnel, I can feel it; my legs can't help but to tense up. It's coming—no way to avoid it, let me wedge my shoulder and arm in-between these rails next to me, clutch the bottom of the seat and brace for it.

Arrrgh!

The ringing.

Shiiii...aaaaah aahhhh aaarrrgggghhhhh

Jarringly, it climbs into my ears with a rush of air that feels like it's eating at my canal. It comes faster than the other times— without warning— already tearing away at my senses.

Need to distract myself, need to read something ...Okay, this colorful poster of a cut-out plane flying over a deep blue cut-out sea is grabbing my attention. It's helping ...

Regardless of the constant shrills that remind me of chalk scrapping across a blackboard, riding over my face to my forehead, I can imagine resting at a beach.

Really can't recall the last time I been to one but Joel from work is always telling me to go. Come to think of it, so are my two personal shrinks: Greg my barber and Carrie my bartender. Carrie always seems to be hinting to me to take her out, but I never been too much into Euro chicks; that's messed up too. She has an alright figure, and she's cool to talk and all but …

Still sometimes I wonder if the mental disease of racism clouds my judgment. *Or could it be my parents warning of changing the charge of my etheric by mixing?*

Greg, on the other hand, says to me that I need to contact Yemoja. Get in touch with Nuwn: the waters. He was raised in the teachings as well. He might be the only one I know that keeps me from going over the deep end.

Plus, he's nice with the clippers. I need to go see him. I'm starting to wolf-out.

Between seeing myself at the beach and thinking about how pitifully small my social life really is, the near unbearable headache pounding down on my head is simmering down. I'm finally able to raise my head, just noticing how much the car filled up with people.

One of them looks a little suspicious.

"Ladies and Gentlemen, I apologize for interrupting you this morning. My name is Eliot." He speaks clearly, even with that raspy smoker's tone leaving his lips. "You don't know me from a hole in the wall."

True. We much prefer the hole. At least that hole don't speak.

"But you must trust me when I say, Directive Living wants your babies—especially the black ones." Without flinching or losing a step in his speech the words callously leave his mouth. I guess he doesn't see *all the Nubians* (Who says Black or African American anymore?) riding in this car and the small number of Euros sprinkled in here and there.

No one pays him attention.

The train and its passengers continue to rock and sway as we barrel through the tunnel at high speeds. Folks are practically glued to their devices, playing their games with droided-out thumbs, or swept into the world of their E-books and Windows. One dude, a teen, not too far away from me, sits slouched over in his seat chanting some hip-hop song in a deep murmur, robotically bopping his head, the rest of his body restricted by his tight clothing. The words are coming out clear enough to make sense to me, but the trance-like rhythm leaving his lips would confuse anyone else. He fidgets all about, looking up with a lemur's curiosity every few seconds, then mindlessly scratches his head.

Yeah, he's high … maybe on sketch.

It's a designer drug that's a mixture of prescription medications and high-end imported ingredients. Just noticed I'm staring at him, trying to figure out how someone like him got a hold of it.

"The fuck you looking at?"

Wow, that was surreal! The way he quickly tugged at his earlobe and shut the music off. He pulls his lip up scrunching the rest of his face. "Well?" He's scowling at me now, the white parts of his eyes crimson— engorged with blood.

"Feelin' your plants, that's all." I respond without missing a beat. "Those the new shits, right?" It's a stupid thing to say, since I can't see the cybernetic implants in his inner ear.

He nods his head at me anyway, too high to realize this. Then, tugging his ear again, drops back into his *trip*. The music is now audible, not blasting, but audible to me. Which means it's at a volume that will damage his ears.

As far as phone-plants go, it will be a clear blue sky in Up-Metro before those things surgically replace my eardrums.

I recall someone at the office saying that they started out as replacements for the hearing impaired and eventually were adapted by corporations as a wireless product.

"You think their pamphlets direct you to better living," Eliot says. "But there are hidden sigils worked into the paper. Sigils that will only direct you into being a *slave.*" Our public griot had less tack than some of those idiots I work with.

But could all that mess he's spitting be true? How many people on this train know what a sigil means? And doesn't he know that Nubians these days don't refer to their kidnapping as Slavery? Or themselves as Slaves?

This tall slender self-stylized prophet chose the correct demographic, but his words are wasted on deaf ears. Our train is headed directly into one of the last densely Nubian populated neighborhoods in the city to be gentrified … Well attempted anyway. And it doesn't seem like there will be any change in the high crime rate (the *supposed* high crime rate), nor the strong solidarity in Nubian homeownership for it to happen.

Funny shit though. Crimes usually involved the assault and robbery of outsiders, extortion of Asian and Euro shop-owners and the distribution of narcotics to tourists … or anyone else brave enough to venture in. And my place of work— the place this man spoke about so intimately about— was dead center in the middle of all that.

"He's *right!*" A slim, mocha-toned young lady yells, jumping up from her seat. "They've been doing questionable tests since Tuskegee—all surrounding Melanin!" Looks like she is about to *go in* before the young woman next to her tugs on her arm and snatches her back into her seat.

"They've been doing this since slavery. And it's not just them—oh believe me. Not just them." Suddenly, Eliot's voice is graver. "This thing goes to a top that no one can ever imagine." He finishes, his breathing erratic and his face dripping with sweat.

As if on cue, sparks shoot up from the tracks in front of the windows, crackling like a bad omen. We are close to the end of the long ride of countless skipped stops. All the stops that go speeding past our eyes—beams of tauntingly dancing long lights—are the *privileged* communities of the city.

Mid-Town.

Kinda' hard to keep thinking about all of this, while a young Nubian boy presses his face against the window, jumping excitedly each time we pass a station.

Not knowing the harsh realities of Mass Gentrification.

"Mommy, so clean! I want to go there!" he bawls out in joy, his face gleaming with excitement.

His mother's face says otherwise.

She knows the truth.

Over the past months, it seems more and more of the people from Up-Metro are being kindly *pushed* away from taking the local. A fare hike for service into Mid-Town here and there, coupled with scheduled construction of track work has done a lot to distract people from the truth.

Living in Down-Metro is a mediocre life, not knowing all the pleasures of Mid-Town and not knowing the blatant racism aimed at Up-Metro. Which is sort of a Black Wall Street throughout all of Brooklyn.

The whole time Eliot is speaking, two large Euros dressed in black are silently, *intently*, watching him from their seats.

And who can't see how they been easing themselves over to him ... Looks like he finally noticed them.

All his boisterous talk and drive has fled. He's timidly making his way over to the doors, seeing his speech hit a sour note.

Attempting to conceal his anxiety, clawing silently at the plexi-glass. A cat cooped up in the house for too long.

As the train pulls into the station and comes to a stop, people lose interest in him. They aren't paying attention to what's happening.

Except the loud young lady and me. We both watch things unfold. I can tell by the intense look on her face that she knows things are headed for a bad turn.

Eliot's leaning up against the door, *pushing* against it. He's practically stumbling out as they slide open. Right before he sprints off, he looks back at me with a cracked tortured smile. It sounded strange when these words popped into my head, but that's exactly what it was.

A cracked tortured smile.

The two guys almost fall over one another getting off the train, picking up the pace to catch Eliot. Sticking super close to him from what I can see—

Damn, can't see them anymore!

\<LAST STOP. EVERYONE PLEASE EXIT THE TRAIN\>

The PA's call is loud— almost demanding.

All of us just hold our seats; a few seniors slouch even further into theirs mustering up defiant smirks across their faces. We were all accustomed to being a little defiant about leaving the train. I mean, hey, it's Up-Metro, that's how we do.

I ain't about to break rank for nobody or nothing … Alright, everybody's getting up.

I almost miss the platform when I step off the train— trying to search for those three. It's almost like second nature. The first being to keep in step with folks in the crowd who appear to be veterans of the area. They're the ones outsiders pays close attention to, and try to stay close to, as they move smoothly through the crowd.

I remember learning this about two years ago, when I escaped a mugging. At that time, I stuck out like a sore thumb. And it didn't help that the dude holding the knife to my throat recognized me as a Social Worker.

Fortunately, an older man who seemed to have some clout, convinced my attacker it wasn't worth it. "Don't stick out. You stick out, you get stuck." Those were his parting words to me.

While many of the youth casually use the word *rape* to express getting robbed or beaten, in Up-Metro they still use the word *juxtd*. They run it on anyone who they think is an outsider.

The three vanish from sight, but the curious part of me still looks around for them, *and* the predators that lurk about on this ramp.

Ahhh, out of the station, crap, cabbies, and runners aggressively swarming me or anyone else who happens to even glance in their direction. Puffs of cold breath from the mouths of people hustling and haggling, dancing about before going to the clouds in the sky. But the people themselves … they all keep a watchful eye on one another from different perspectives.

As usual, the atmosphere of this place takes me a moment to get used to, no matter how many times I come out here, which must be well over a thousand by now.

There is something in the air distinctly… *Nubian.*

Some way or another when I'm out here in Up-Metro around Nubian people, my skin begins to feel electrified, especially in busy areas.

Can't explain it. It just is. *Like a spreading field of energy. And only the people of Up-Metro seem to know about it in-depth… Some I hear can manipulate it.*

The scattered coves of trees nestling brownstones, that appeared to blend into public parks, gives Up-Metro a suburban look. Especially with the building height regulation of no more than four stories high.

The Directive Living complex is only four stories.

Still the city manages to construct housing communities, *projects,* here and there outside the limits. Then there are the "building code wars" between downtown Up-Metro property owners and the City Council of Mid-Town. So, with all this going on no one can see, or maybe some don't want to acknowledge, an actual BLACK POWER evolving in Up-Metro.

9:20am

Emil waves at me from his cart like he always does and, although my head doesn't turn in his direction while walking past him…somehow, he *knew* that I saw him.

Need to keep it moving though, ignore the flash of aluminum wrap out of the corner of my eye.

Completely forgetting about work and the several blocks needed to get there, I find myself turning around to see him standing there waiting for me. He's doing nothing else but twisting the wrap side to side to reflect the sun's rays in my face; the rolling gleam seems to be screaming, "Breakfast!"

It's too tempting to ignore.

There's enough time to get a sandwich and still get into work to take a shower … yeah. I have a few extra regulation suits in my locker, so I won't get penalized for lacking a uniform.

What the—?

Toni's lifeless body, her limbs twitching and lacking in color, flashed in front of my eyes. The people I staggered into gently pushed me back to my feet.

It's coming again, snapping like camera flashes— nearly blinding me. I nearly stumble into Emil, who immediately scrunches up his face and rubs his nose. Did he catch wind of all the scents that must be soaked into my skin and clothing?

So, 'noid right now. Are any of those scents coming at him, rank-smelling of death? There's no way to tell just by looking at him. It's too difficult to read into his cheerfulness.

Aw man … again.

Fresh bruises on his cheeks look wedged into his thick beard, but he's still smiling and shit. He's been hit-up for rent *again*. Never asked him about it, but it's clear he's giving his hard-earned money to thugs in this sector.

Can they really be considered the thugs in Novus?

The more I look at him, the more there is to be seen in his appearance … about what he's going through. Whatever awkward silence that's building up between us snaps along with the brown paper bag he joyfully pops open. The distinct sound of the aluminum-wrapping sliding across the inside of the bag was his trademark when serving folks, as his reader clicked away from your chunk.

But we never talked.

I always think about that each time I see him. I never ordered what I want; he always just gives me what he thinks I want. That's how it's been from the first time ordering with him.

It's getting late—need to be out of here.

"Take care of yourself."

Wait a minute, did he just talk to me?

Is this him speaking in a gruff-ass voice? It's strange because Emil never talked to *anybody*. I mean, it didn't stop people from having a fulfilling conversation with him, when they saw they could just yammer on until their order was finished. Whatever motivated him to speak today definitely helps to lift my spirits.

Okay, got the sub snuggly underneath my arm, now my gloveless hands can go into my pockets.

What's this burning sensation literally chewing at my neck?

The corner light just changed to green, but whatever is boring into me is too much for me not to look back. My head literally is turning on its own … digging my chin slowly into my shoulder as my glare takes in everyone who is walking near me.

Emil sticks out in a sea of dark complexion people.

There he is, looking at— no *staring* at— me from the distance, still in the same position I left him in.

What's up with him?

Thick hairy forearms rest across his stomach while his eyes look frozen in space…but away from the rest of his body. Just floating there as if they were glowing in darkness or something. I don't know why this dude never wears a jacket when its brick out.

"We good?" *Why'd I say that?* Calling out to him and throwing up my hands might be seen as aggressive. That and the bass in my voice.

The teens passing me are turning to look in our direction, which is probably their perception: I was beefin' at Emil. One of them, the skinniest out of the bunch, abruptly taps his boy to stop while the others followed suit.

"Yo!" He stretches the 'o' as far as he can to emphasize his swag. "You got a problem with that Euro sandwich-making mofo ova' there?"

Damn, his breath smells harsh! And what's with the uninvited hand on my shoulder? His grubby little fingers are digging themselves into the wool of my jacket. Immediately I catch all the dirt lodged in their nails. *He's probably been on the streets for a while now.*

I'm just about to brush his hand off me—before the thick tribal bow tattoo in the crux of his thumb grabs my attention.

Nine Bows.

"See something scary?"

His chuckling gets me a bit worried. *But you not going to lay another hand on my shoulder.*

"Oh, you want to move all around and shit, ight OG." He's getting frustrated.

Well maybe now is better than any other time to thump.

"Now, one more time. Is this death-dissing mayo-fuck, giving you a problem?" His voice, now irritated, returning to the trigger question.

He's not going to do anything.

At least not to me.

That scrawny hand of his nervously slides off me, yet he nimbly grabs the thick smoking blunt passed to him, knocking off a bit of ash from it. The long draw he takes cracks into the air with embers sparking out at me.

"Nah, he okay." I hope he believes those words that came flying out my mouth in between his pulls. I'm doing my best not to take in the large puff of smoke floating by me.

"Yeah?" He's not convinced. Turning to a short dude next to him, he passes off the rest of *the-permanent-vacation-if-I-inhaled* to him. "Yo' kill that son; bout to put in some work." Morality is absent from the tone of his voice and it like shifts the whole mood.

He can't be no more than fifteen to sixteen years old, at the most, but that tattoo burned into his skin adds years of cold-heartedness to his age.

I don't want to see Emil get his ass whooped over something that still isn't clear to me. Glancing cautiously, slowly, back at him while these dudes were pumping each other up I see Emil's arms still crossed. He's looking directly at us.

What's wrong him? Emil stop that dumb shit you doing! I'm late for work and smell like all sorts of things standing out here.

The cold air that's been keeping me clear-headed and alert, slowly sinks pass the thick blanket of fear around me, into my skin chilling my muscles and nerves. Personal safety and iron bars quickly goad me to turn away and cross the street when the glimpse of the green light catches my attention.

And that's what I am going to do.

Without looking back, keep making your way to the other side of the street; ignore the trembling of your body and—the cries of Emil.

His thick Mediterranean accent wails out loudly through the streets, pass calamity of the vehicles in the early day rush. Routine Up-Metro extortion is exacting its payment from him.

This is the third time today I ignored someone in need—for my own sake.

I feel like crap.

The overpass, that leads to Directive Living, draws ominously closer and closer to me … I never felt more alone. Well, there it is, an empty scrip bottle, followed by others littered about along the sides of the overpass.

I'm at work.

Catching a chill and this sandwich keeps slipping from underneath my arm. It's hard to keep it clutched closer to my ribs and stop my body heat from escaping.

This next shot of bitter cold smashing against my face is difficult to push against. I can't help thinking it's preparing me for the set of crap I'll have to deal with at work.

The craziness is the weird sound the wind makes when it barrels across the path, tearing into me like it doesn't give a damn about the type of morning I had.

It's whispering, *"Leave here…"* I swear that is what it sounds like.

"Hey scab," Waves calls out to me. "When you gonna come work for us, huh?"

Not in the mood for his mess, I speed up my pace.

As usual, there are folks loitering all over the three blocks of bridge, most of them involved with DL in one of two ways: Patients or Dealers.

Waves held down most of it with his flamboyant-ass workers spread out all through the stretch of bridge, his insects swarming anyone that came near them. One guy, skinnier than the one who set in on Emil, keeps pestering a boy walking with his head down, moping down the path, a lanky-looking cat waddling in skin tight jeans looking flashy as hell. It seems Waves isn't schooling his workers, or just doesn't care.

The Dealers sit about all day, looking to buy medications from patients to sell to out-of-towners, Mid-City Folk, and the occasional Euro Police Officer.

It's big money.

Only those who were in The Life and categorized as *African American* ever got the real prescriptions. Everybody else was doled out placebos or routine psychotherapy. Whoever arrived on the daily to monthly schedule to receive prescriptions became a prime resource for legal and illegal currency earning potential, preyed upon by Health Care Providers and Street-Thugs alike.

"C'mon leave me alone. I don't have scrips." The young man being stalked does his best to push the dude all in his pockets away …timidly yelling out, hoping someone will come to his aid.

He's one of my cases, another one in need—that will be ignored by me. Oh shit, should have been paying attention to my surroundings! There's my supervisor's getting out his Tesla, need to dip around to the back entrance.

I really hate coming back here and pressing my face up to the smudged-up entrance scanner, hearing that familiar click pop the door open. *Glad I had these wet naps in my pocket. The scanners smell horrible—who knows what someone left on the scanner? What the hell? Why is my heart is starting to race—? Time to punch in.*

It's 10:00.

Chapter 3

Earlier

8:00am

"Hurry up, Heifer." With her less than flattering name for me, Josie's voice briskly seeps through our bedroom door.

And me being me, I allowed myself to be pulled out of my meditation by it. My last *Aum*, that was having some degree of success ridding my bones of their frailty, broke in mid-chant. It took me *hours* to get my body back in some reasonable working order for the day and now it seemed all wasted. The aches are returning, hitting my knees first then riding into my back.

Someone please, I need guidance! How do I manage my body—the way it is now?!

"Josie!" Yeah, I'm yelling. Why control my anger? Oh, because you'll strain your voice—*oowwww*.

A split second, that's how long it took for my entire body to smack my mind with the sensation of blocked oxygen. *But I am still breathing.*

The entire room is flying right in front of me, along with the statue of Sakhumtat resting on the altar. Trying to follow it with my eyes, just to keep myself from spitting up, only makes me dizzier.

"Josie! Josie, come—come help me!"

Something is driving itself into the base of my neck, sending electrical jolts upwards scraping at my skull. Darkness is coming no matter how hard I struggle to keep my lids open. No light, just darkness. Something that I have come to see as a close friend these past w—

"Wake up! Wake up Maffie!"

Josie, please stop calling out to me! And quit patting my face; it's just about numb!

It's a strain to push away that last pat. And even more of a struggle to look up at her. I feel disorientated being on her lap instead of my meditation cushion.

"Again?" My voice is so meek … and tired.

"Again." Worry fills her voice as she answers. "Well, let's get your ass up now." She speaks exasperatedly, doing a horrible job of concealing her concern.

Without another word, Josie stands up too quick with me and the things upsetting in my stomach now want to fly out my mouth.

She's still angry with me, about more than one thing. "Careful with me." Is it the only thing I can manage to get out my mouth without throwing up?

It makes me tight that I'm not strong enough to do anything else but get dragged across the room by her.

"You need to see someone. A— "

"A doctor? A priest? A *what?*" I can't help breaking in viciously with my words, meaning to sting her. *Oh, damn.* Her hands are shaking underneath me while she turns up her face, letting me down gently on the couch.

Sigh.

I really didn't mean to hurt her, but she keeps telling me the same thing. She *knows* none of these people can do anything for me.

There is no illness in me. There is no spirit possessing my mind *or soul* for that matter. The way she just switches up her demeanor and lays her hand tenderly on my face before looking deep into my eyes, makes up for the uneasiness streaming off her body. Her big brown pools are penetrating me while her arms draw me into her chest.

Everything in me wants that; limply my arms catch her waist. My fingers struggle to clasp together to latch onto her. There's literally no strength in my arms to hold her on my own. Sitting silently in each other's arms, is calming. I sense my insides less on fire and my bones stronger … less brittle.

Why?

Maybe it's this old couch we both dragged here from Up-Metro, still comfortable as the day we were first *together* on it. *Caught together on it.*

The day we were kicked out my mother's house and forced to take, "that God-awful thing" with us. I often wondered how God and awful were so easily fit together by Mom. But luckily for us, we had money saved up and vacancy in Down-Metro was never an issue.

When you have money.

But those memories drift away with each beat of Josie's heart thumping welcomingly into my ear. *Burying my face in her breasts feels like the only way I can get more healing from her. My attack is over ... silently taking strength from her to continue to settle my bones.*

It's not the couch. It's me taking from Josie.

The comforting *Sigh* leaves both our lips, almost in unison.

"Thanks, Josie." I mean every word of it ... warmly.

"I got you, Bae!" She bawls out with equal sentiment along with her enthusiasm.

"C'mon, our food is getting cold." She's being kind of rough getting me to my feet, literally dragging me down the hall—can barely catch my breath.

Thank goodness for the warmth we built into our apartment gently caressing my body, as we make our way to the kitchen, everything in its walls and floors reach out to greet me.

Our home ...

Coming into the kitchen, I am welcomed by my favorite early day sounds: The O Channel gently taking my ears captive. Our *Window* pulsing out vivid projections as clear and *juicy* as the new upgrade could provide. The angle of its screen follows our position with programmed faithfulness, providing us with our own personal views.

"I can walk on my own now, Josie."

"You sure?"

"Yes." *Ohh these kitty-slippers Josie got me are soooo warm inside, got me shuffling over to my counter seat all childlike.*

The weather report practically jerks me out my little cute-with-me moment.

<Recent RP EVENT claims 13 as CME causes minimal property damage to Novus City>
<Please report to your local DL Auxiliary Unit if you need to schedule a therapeutic session>

"Josie, are you hearing this? You noticed it?" *Maybe that RP Event had something to do with my more than challenging time in the early rising ... an almost pulling sensation.*

"Nah, my melanin was popping for a whole other reason." She would answer me that way.

<Today's temperature is 35 degrees F. Clear skies in Mid-Town and Down-Metro>

<And now for Up-Metro. Cloudy skies with patches of sun; strong chance of thunderstorms>

The announcement broke and returned to O.

"Damn!" Josie let out, taking her seat. She's almost numb to hearing the **RP EVENT** report.

As for me, I joyously climb into mine. *I'm looking forward to the air cleansing rain to sweep through Novus.*

I turn my attention to my Quinoa; the aroma has been steaming deliciously into my nose for the past few minutes. It's time to give thanks.

Okay, need to slowly allow a bit of *myself* to extend into my fingertips and contact the food, its warmth and *information* calmly relay back up through my senses. *Eeaaasy*…just as slow, bring my ancestors to mind or else the connection will break up. And I won't eat.

I can't eat.

Alright … got it. And I'm done.

Ever since that Saturday about three weeks ago, it's been frustrating how my body will go into paralysis until I performed that ritual before eating, a ritual that I woke up knowing without anyone telling me.

Mmmmmmm ... those few hearty spoonfuls wiped away my daydreaming, bringing me back to the present. Okay, eating finally. I can't help this natural feeling of wanting to break into a little breakfast dance.

I must look like a damned fool.

Josie keeps cutting glances at me while sticking her knife and fork into a large chunk of breakfast sausage. I'm simultaneously stealing looks at her mid-drift with mild scorn across her face.

She's just now getting the piece and size of sausage she wants on her fork, shoving it all into her mouth. I love her, but she has no table manners whatsoever. The few chews she gives to each bite echo irritatingly into my ears, and my sensitivity literally has me hearing each of those partially bitten morsels struggle down her throat.

Every gulp rings out so loud I *feel* it get lodged in my own throat, then forced down.

I'm almost choking on my own food.

Wait.

Something is not right. Why is my plate filled with cut-up sausages? What's happening? Why am I being pulled *into her consciousness?*

She hasn't noticed.

Bit by bit I manage to pull myself free, without her finding out. It's like being *glued* to her senses. Her experience. Ugh ... my senses are starting to become my own again. Meanwhile, Josie is really working that last bit of syrup into a piece of pancake and sausage smooshed together on her fork, and her doing a little breakfast dance of her own.

Yup, here we are, calming down from our passive aggressions, doing our little dances watching O—and running late. The sun is coming directly through the window. I don't need to check the clock on the wall.

8:30am

"Shit!" It's crazy the way she jumps off the stool, kebabs another piece of pancake and sausage and runs for the bedroom.

Yeah, we're late.

Josie needs to be at the restaurant in the next 30 minutes. It doesn't look like their head-chef is going to be on time today. And me, I must drop off some papers at school, go to Directive Living, then prepare for this evening's meeting. Rather than run about like a chicken with no head, I am going to continue to eat my food as if nothing else matters, savoring every bit of crunchy walnut and agave mixed into it.

Josie can really throw down.

"Hurry up with the damn kahnauh and get your clothes on." Josie hammers out, hopping on one leg trying to put her foot through her pants leg.

"It's pronounced *keen-wah* and I'm already dressed." I swirl around in my chair and tug at my sweat suit.

I know that makes her angry.

"Heifer." It slips out from underneath her breath. She finally manages to get her pants on.

Well, neither of us are going to wash our plates, let me at least put them in the sink and squeeze some dish-liquid on them. I hardly want to get up from my seat, but at least my body—especially my bones—feel much better.

"Nah girl, don't put none of that fake so-called environmental-safe shit on my plate," Josie says. "You know better. Put the *real* liquid, I brought on it." She's starting up her mess now. looking to beat me at getting ready through distraction.

"Yeah well, who cares? I see you're ready now." Snapping back at Josie like that can lead to a long-winded battle, but this time, she just smugly zips up her jacket.

Bundling up in this puffy yellow bubble goose she brought for me last year, Josie can't see me sneaking glances at her, looking all rugged in the hugging black leatherjacket I brought for her.

"Oh, the window!"

Wow, never seen her sprint like that to the kitchen just to peer in and blink to snap the window down. What's up with her?

Her dashing back though, then trying to quickly place her hand on the palm seal, got completely shut down when it didn't respond right away.

"Hurry up, we're late!" I barked. *We need to get a move on.*

The blank look on her face somehow froze everything around us. She broke *that* by slamming her hand against the seal—nothing happened. Now she's just banging against it.

"Josie!"

"WhaaaaAt!?"

Okay, I'm in for it.

<Block Open>

Whew! That's a relief! It opened just before things could pop off.

"Could you see yourself to moving out the way?" Josie's acting real funny right now, blocking me from the palm seal so I can't lock the door.

"I got it." I daintily place my hand on the seal.

She's giving me duck-lips while I'm doing it.

<Block Secured>

As we rushed down the corridor, I see all the usual squatters still huddled up the corners, their stale musk briefly making my eyes tear. We both ignore the faint shuffling sound a flight below us, flying down the stairs avoiding the empty scrip bottles in our way.

Oh shit, Mr. Jameson, where did he come from?

Josie almost runs over him.

"Wee Bastards!"

He wants to cuss at us and wave his cane, losing his balance while he's trying to air us out. Lucky for him, he's able to catch on to the banister just before he falls.

"Have a good day Mr. Jameson," we say in unison.

Without stopping, we go even faster, skipping more and more steps. Three, then five at a time, almost tripping, our shoes—her low heels and my boots—clacking out loud echoes through the stairwell. Great, we're in the lobby; we're able to bolt out the door together just as someone comes in.

Freaking palm seals slow people up.

"Come on Maffie, *move!* The 9:00am will be there soon." She's really got a good grip on my arm, pulling me along with her.

Ahhhh…my stomach is beginning to cramp up. With each step my food swishes around, the little that is in there anyway. But I am going to keep up with Josie. For goodness' sake, I will.

With the way things are going, her tongue was the last thing that needed to be lashing out at me. Okay, we're at the main overpass. I can catch my breath, as we gently corral into the mass of people.

Everyone who barreled into the station ends up being pressed body to body and forced to shuffle in slow.

<Up-Metro Express arriving in one minute>

People around us are clearing their eyes, some even using drops. We're lucky to live close to the stop before the junction. However, it was only good if you were going to Up-Metro. But then again no one left Down-Metro to go into Mid-Town much anyway … or maybe never at all.

"Get your Chunking ready!" One Handler bellows as others chime in as they appear from their scattered booths, searching for anyone who would be Double-Backing the Eye-Scan.

A moment of anxiety is hitting me. *Damn, damn,* damn. *Okay, got to stop rubbing my eyes and just try to remember the last time they were chunked. Let's see, I been going back and forth this whole week and…*

"You're okay."

Okaaay, she could have asked first before peeling back my eyelid. Chunks are loaded onto a minute disk attached around the cornea, so how could she see to know anyway?

"Yeah, you have about eight more left."

She really has me wondering.

"Alright Maffie, I can't take the suspicious look you're giving me. Remember the money that was supposed to go to my new uniform? Well, I spent it on a Chunking Upgrade."

"Josie wh—"

"Never mind, I can wait another week or month. At least I can read both our Chunking and get fare discounts."

But her current uniform can't take anymore hemming.

It's bad enough that it was mandatory for everyone to have the disc surgically implanted, but to give into more procedures for the sake of comfort …

Oh Josie!

Guess this will have to hold until later. The train's pulling in, screeching something terrible, tearing up the people's ears while throwing sparks out wildly. Down-Metro folk have been known to have a high case of tinnitus and other hearing issues.

Look at this now. People coughing all up and down the platform. Many of them just about to spit— knowing very well they better not.

The occasional track fires and lack of proper maintenance has caused more than its share of breathing problems. Their *solution* was to enforce strict laws on littering which neither protects the passengers nor assumes responsibility for the results of their own actions.

Nevertheless, we all line up impatiently at the markers, which are just far enough for people to avoid getting hit by the train, but close enough for them to breathe in tainted air waiting for the doors to open.

<Prepare for Scan>

Everyone shuffles forward almost mindlessly, but still make sure they keep their places in line. During these times, it was only natural for Josie and I turn to one another and nod, our way of letting each other know we are alert. I keep a watch on the people in front of me and shift side to side while we continue forward.

Stay in the moment.

"Why the hell you nudged me like that?" Josie's barking softly, turning up her face... *When she should just be picking up on my cue.*

"Someone's about to try. Oh shit, it's this one in front of us, right?" she whispered. Where was she at in her head, to whisper naively into my ear like that?

Now you want to be less conspicuous.

She's backing us away from them quietly.

"Yes, these two right here. They're going to do it." *Why am I almost giggling this into her ear as I whisper?*

But folks around us are not as discreet. *Look at how many of them slip out their cellphones.*

I can tell a lot of them are fumbling around deleting files to make space. Others are rubbing their temples, deleting files from their I-Plants. These two men in front of us, one tall and stout, the other slim and of medium height, both Euro, are beginning to make their move. By the looks of their clothing and their mannerisms, they are probably out-of-towners, maybe from out of the country.

The stout one's goes in first, immediately hugged tightly by his friend from behind. Clumsily, the slim one tries to mirror his friend's steps, pressing his forehead to his partner's neck— trying to fit as close to him as possible.

Double-Backing. Probably picked up from someone from Up-Metro.

Probably dumber than the name given to it and at the same time the bravest thing to do on the Metro Line.

Ninety percent of the time it never works.

We were about to see firsthand and up-close the same mess we saw yesterday.

"Stand back!" Josie almost knocks me down.

Two freakishly huge Handlers came charging through people, blasting curses inconsiderately into everyone's face before they're knocked out the way. Without warning, one of them swings out a bulk of an arm at the smaller Euro, who almost passes out (when he sees it) before carrying his head then body off the train. He goes flying into the other Handler's chest, sliding down, and falling sloppily to the platform floor.

His accomplice now decides to whip around quicker than the weight of his body could manage and clumsily throws his hands up. "I am sorry! We are out of town! We were robbed and no money!" he sobs, stumbling to speak properly, then turns his head to look down at his partner sprawled under a Handler's boot. "Please, please we are from other country! We did not know! We did not *knoo-oo-ooo!*" As the last, o' leaves his lips, the Handler smacks him in the face; it goes from a swarthy complexion to beet red in seconds.

"Get your ass off the platform," the other Handler speaks unsympathetically, while dragging him by the collar.

Who's this chick standing up?

It's a young Euro lady looking angry as hell. "You can't treat him like that. He's not from here," she pleads. "Please be rational." Strain is all up in her voice.

"Bitch shut up and sit your ass down, before you mark yourself in Up-Metro," he snaps at her harshly.

Wasting no time, she slinks down into her seat, the look on her face now meek and helpless.

I know that's right.

It seems she knows his words, as cold as they are, are truthful. A bit of my heart goes out to her.

Lately the Handlers were becoming brutal in their approach, disgruntled about their service contracts. It was all over The Windows the past week. Their term contract of work did not pay them by the hour, nor week. It was one lump sum locking them in work for a season, regardless of their funds being rapidly depleted by the cost of living.

They must hate their job.

Forced to expel anyone off the train, no matter age, or their condition, must do something to their morality. And one day, after seeing one of them chewed out by their superiors, I knew they couldn't feel supported in any way.

So, I guess, yes, they abuse their power. Some were also locked into Constellation 13.

"Maffie!"

Why is Josie tugging at my sleeve?

"Maffie, stop daydreaming, you may start pulling again." That warning made me nervous. "I'm alright. Let's get in." I was doing my best to ignore the pin-size *hole* in front of me that slowly closed.

She doesn't notice. But is she referring to earlier, or in general?

As usual, the scanner's noisily re-setting abruptly blinded me, taking my stored credit. A little dazed, but none for worse, and like yesterday (and days before), we find ourselves both rubbing our eyes and heading for seats to the back near the conductor.

Josie's changing her demeanor quick, fitting into the role of an a Up-Metroer. Slumping over a bit and letting her elbows rest on her thighs, tensing her cheeks, and pushing a little attitude into her lips. And me, all I do is *think* of the qualities and project that energy. For all the trips to Up-Metro and waitressing at clubs, there was hardly a time when that attitude was not *absorbed* by me.

Intentionally or Unintentionally.

But, unlike Josie, I could never bring myself to hold my body that way.

Ahhh, c'mon…not now. Pain is creeping back up into my joints. I need more time to recover.

I'm starting to drift … gravity pulling me down into the *bubbliness* of my coat, my senses unfolding the world I see in front of me. Everybody is checking each other out and switching up how they sit and how their faces stand out. It would be a long ride before we reached Up-Metro, but people always treated the actual train ride like being there. So much tension, so much fear with mixtures of defiance sits thick in the air, filling the car.

Misty … reds … blues … of small electrical currents…aggressive air currents rubbing against my fa--

<DUE TO NECESSARY TRACK WORK THIS TRAIN WILL BE GOING OUT OF SERVICE>

"WTF!" a big guy in a correction's uniform yells out.

At least that sudden outburst takes my focus off the things around me. Normally when an angry person on the train causes a ruckus it doesn't draw me in as much because I shield myself from their projections.

That much I did learn how to do.

Something about this guy isn't right. All that fidgeting with his duffle bag and whispering to himself. There's a bad aura about him.

But the *spirit* about him is familiar.

Ohhhh, knots tying up in my stomach … faint voices stirring in my head. Got to hide it from Josie.

<NEXT STOP PLEASE TRANSFER FOR THE CONNECTING TRAIN>

It's strange the way he rushes for the doors, hitting them with clenched hands. Whipping his head towards everyone, then quickly turning it back to hide his face.

"C'mon, *c'mon!*" Now banging on the windows incessantly.

We are pulling into the stop. Folks are paying this guy no mind. The doors are starting to slide open, but not fast enough for him—he darts out, dragging his duffle bag behind him.

From one side of the platform to the other, all of us passengers left the train, a rushing wave of people, stop short of crashing over into the tracks.

My stomach's starting to settle along as well as the aches in my joints and that strange guy is … elsewhere …

Away from me.

Our connecting train lazily teeters into the station from side to side, as if it didn't really want to fill its body up with a pack of strangers. Groups of folks come just about cheek to cheek to one another, while others keep their distance with standoffish attitudes. Back and forth, different currents of soul pressure (the best way I can describe it) swirl about and sweep through the air. All of them brushing up against me, the strongest of them seeking entry.

Insisting much more strongly than earlier.

Josie's pulling me closer to her and placing a much-needed kiss on my neck. It was at these times when I didn't mind our height difference; her body wrapped around mine like a security blanket.

"Seats!" Josie broke out when the door slid open.

Splitting up, pushing, and nudging, we got the seats we wanted. And as usual we took two seats in the back of the car next to the conductor. But we rudely dash in front of a middle-aged couple who eyed them first. As soon as we sat down and let the packs off our backs, the couple scrunched up their faces at us while hugging the pole in front of them.

"We should give them our seats," I spoke softly to Josie, so as not to be heard.

"Maffie, relax. You stand up for the entire ride when you should be sitting and watch how fast you'll be held by Directive Living," she said this with all sorts of seriousness, hunching over on my legs. Now gripping the inside of my thigh firmly and graduating to stroking it.

It feels good.

Not that it turns me on or anything like that, it just feels *good*. I want her there, close to me, but I am sure that Josie was leading elsewhere with it …leaning slyly over to my neck, nibbling her way up to my ear, leaving gentle kisses all over my skin.

"Stop it Josie—we are on the train for goodness' sake." Moving away from her lips like this probably frustrates her.

"Why should I?" she says teasingly. "No one cares *what* we do." Her guile is sweet and soft like her breath, breathing her last word onto my neck before her lips pressed against it.

I'll just lay my hand on her cheek, let my fingers gently caress it then pull away … Oh damn. I did it now.

The muscles in her face are tensing lightly against my palm. *Whoa!* We're beginning a ride through a rough patch of tracks.

"Maffie … I—"

The train jerks sharply and my arm flies up—I wind up slapping her by accident. It was loud enough for everyone on the train to hear, but not one head turned in our direction.

"Well, *damn* then. I guess actions do speak louder than words," Josie tries to mutter spitefully, but grins all the while …

Typical.

Why me? Awww c'mon Josie don't throw yourself back in the seat that way. You're still trying to maintain some swag in your disposition. Oh Josie.

"I apologize Josie, it was the train and—"

"Save it."

Why is she carrying on and waving her hand all stiff, shooing me away?

"You need to stay focused about your appointment … and avoiding Constellation 13."

"You're right," I agree, brought back to the reality of being seriously focused about my appointment.

Suddenly all the busy chatter of people and the disturbing gear-grinding noise of the train grows faint—why did my ears just pop?

What's this vacuum of silence closing-in around my head? Nothing's giving off a sound, can't panic…don't panic. Everything is beginning to move through space softly—no sound attached. Oh, no … I can't even hear the lub-dub, lub-dub of my heartbeat; only feel it. Why can't I? I should.

Wait. Head is getting hot; it's in my neck now…what's this weird heat passing over me, passing down my legs, finally resting into my feet.

Someone is watching me.

Somewhere on the train, they're staring or sending their intentions at me. Stop struggling to remain calm, just search the train (it may just be nothing). Look for anyone whose glance or minor soul pressure matches up with the energy I'm receiving.

There *is* one person. The man sitting at the far end in one of the side chairs.

But he's not paying me any attention.

It's not him. How about these other folks —although it's still better to watch him from my peripheral vision? He seems uneasy in his seat, keeps moving about, sticking his arms in and out of the bars next to him.

Finally. Bit by bit, sound is returning to my ears. I can hear my heartbeat again.

I'm doing my best to observe him without being noticed, especially by Josie. But our eyes still meet. For him, it was a passing glance but for me—

It's something different.

Wherever our eyes connected in the space between us, tracked back into my chest and got my heart to pounding…more than it already was.

Oh geez, cramping in my chest, getting tight, things and people becoming blurred shapes. Not now. Not here. I am going to pull.

Before Josie sees me having another *attack,* got to silently perform a few breathing locks, lower my neck engage my diaphragm…see the stillness of my sympathetic system, keep my neck from cranking down.

"Hey, Maffie …" She's looking at me funny; my head's throbbing even more.

"Maffie." Her hands gripping mine so tight, she's almost breaking them …

Again.

Now, the gentle taps of my pulse, that I worked *so* hard for, flip right back to a pounding pouring into my head without restraint.

What's with Josie's soul pressure?

It's starting to get agitated.

"Maffie, oh *shit!*"

Her worry is messing with the pitch of her voice, the sound is stinging my eardrums, can't stop my head from falling in-between my legs.

Yow! Things in my stomach riding up into my throat. Can hardly raise my head, keep getting struck with lightheadedness followed by gagging … forcing me back down between my knees.

All I can do is stare at the floor and try to keep things down, while the thick and heavy *wah-wah wah-wah* sound washes around in my head.

Images coming to mind … almost projecting right in front of me … a dark lit room, damp … and a drain?

Josie's hand gliding smoothly across my back literally wiped away the beginnings of what was literally a hologram forming in front of me. *Why did she have to include gentle strokes along my hips, tho'?*

Whatever's blocking up tension in my upper-chest and stomach is breaking up. The stagnate flow of energy, now released, rushed down into the rest of my body, flushing everything in its path. And the swaying of the train along with Josie's caressing is bringing my frequency back to normal.

Sigh…normal.

"Maffie …" Her energy is coming off less distressed. Her soul pressure is still crackling out, but lower in frequency. "I really thought you were going to pull right here."

I always meant to ask if all this has any effect on her.

"Josie!" it feels like I'm yelling, but I am barely able to talk. She doesn't hear me; the train is hitting a stretch of noisy track. "JOSIE!" *Oh no. I'm sure to lose my voice, but at least she heard me.*

"Yes, Maffie." Glad she is leaning over to me with her full attention.

"Is the food ordered?" That came out timid, even though I want to be silent more than anything else.

I really need to know that is done.

"Yes. Yes, it is." Her answer was *all that* and her soul pressure is calm now.

"Good." *I'm happy now.*

But what's with this strange looking Euro springing up from his seat, just when the sense of peace started to pass all through my body?

"Ladies and Gentlemen, I apologize for interrupting you this morning."

8:45am

Chapter 4

The Office

Fuuuckkk.

Another day of pushing papers from one side of my desk to the other, then pushing the people attached to those papers from out of the worn chair in front of me through the door. Well, out from the walls of the cubicle dividers anyway. Time to move a few things around my desk ...

And there is my sandwich in the center of surrounding hills of paper holding the mountains of paper behind it at bay—huh? is that my old yoga mat in the corner of my cubicle collecting dust?

So, what.

Thoughts of Buddha and skinny tree-huggers are quickly fading from my thoughts; the sandwich made by Emil is too good to focus on anything else.

Did he survive that beating?

Regardless of this burning in my chest, *whatever that is*, I still scoff down more. Why? Just to wash it down with soda when the chunks want to stay lodged in my throat.

Am I living correctly?

Okay, 10am, time to receive my first *client*… Mafdet Ra? *That can't be her name, at least not legally anyway.*

Let's see orphaned at seven, in and out of foster homes. No record of parents. Nothing. History of Hypertension and early signs of Osteoporosis. *So young to have that.*

There are some things in here that are just freakin' shady. Eight years of no recorded events. Says here that she is currently staying with a slightly older woman, late twenties. The two co-habit a small apartment in Down-Metro and …

Okay I read enough. "Calling #FT001!" *Geez, my voice sounds like I am over-worked sitting in a drive-through window.*

Click.

That's the sixth click of my portable heater, and there's still barely any warmth coming from it at all. Throwing my sweater back on and turning up my collar got me lost in thought, just wandering.

What's going on?

Wait a minute, did a lot of things just happen? And I am unaware of any of it … how long have I been staring at the brilliant red coils of the heater? Wtf, none of its heat is getting to me. Every time I want to pull away from watching it, my intentions are wiped from my thoughts. *And what's with the air, becoming thick around me— pushing against me. Awww c'mon, word?*

Why the fuck are little waves of heat, NOT FROM THE HEATER, becoming visible in front of me?

Red glowing. Spinning together.

They're merging …forming a face, a woman's face with soft features. Need to force my head up to look away from it and see if anyone else in their cubicle is going through something similar—I can't do it. I can't even yell out.

Some *force* is keeping my head locked in place, a big-ass hand vice-grip on my neck. Whatever it is, it's making sure I don't miss how depth slowly fills in the specter-like head floating in front of me.

Fuck just let me move, but the only thing that's moving about is the chill running up and down my spine. My scalp's starting to tingle, going between being on fire then blasted with cold. this is really happening. Oh, shit this is…

Why do you curse so much Peter?

…Wait a minute…who are y—

"Sir?" A woman's voice calling out to me.

"Sir?" When she spoke again, that strange thing in front of me, released whatever hold it had on my eyes—then withered away.

I'm finally, able to move once more.

"Have a seat … uh… Miss Ra." Shi—, at least I could look directly at her. I feel almost robotic motioning to the chair in front of me. I want to laugh so bad, relieved that I still could or want to.

Only a few people I knew went as far as to have a Kemetic name as a *legal name*. Then again, my parents tried to pull that same thing with my name.

So, who is this ski-jacket with legs walking into my cubicle? Her slim young body almost fully engulfed by the bright bubbled sleeves and bulk. And who does she think she is, looking down at the chair with disgust, dusting it off with her scarf before she sits down?

There's something familiar about her. Then it hits me.

She's from the train.

"You're that girl from the train, right?" was just about to leave my lips before I catch myself.

"May I call you by your first name, Mafdet?" I'm familiar with this name and pronounced it as eloquently as I could. "So, did I get your name right?" I push a bit of snugness in my voice, but I'm a little jealous that she has a big jacket on to keep her warm.

Why did I leave mine in my locker? We should be able to keep our personal things … on our person.

"Yes, you did," her tone is curt and disinterested.

"So …" I'm pausing, distracted by more random thoughts, "it says here you're attending community college and wait tables part-time. That's good." I made sure to put a bit of encouragement in my tone.

"I hate this."

Although this is said under her breath, I hear it. *Brush it off.* Here comes the part of my job that's slowly making me less than human each time—with each question.

"Have you any need for a medical evaluation, physical or mental?" I want to stop, but my *vacation* is on the line.

And my possible escape from a murder charge.

"No," her voice is lifeless.

"Do you practice safe sex?" I ask casually, reaching for my sandwich to take another bite…*to make it look casual.*

She is just sitting there with her mouth open, looking like she is about to speak, but now staring sharply at me eating. "What is that you are eating?" She breaks in—with an attitude.

Tearing out another bite looking her dead in the eye, the image of a lion eating his meal then being disturbed by a hyena flashes through my thoughts. Chewing the mess out my food until it gets gummy in between my teeth, the none of your business response waits impatiently on my lips making it difficult to chew.

"It's Bologna and Cheddar Cheese." bits of crust and meat fly out my mouth on the 'b' and 'ch'.

The stoic look on her face slightly flinches each time a piece lands on her.

This one is strange.

The longer I look at her, the more I want this meeting to end because I keep seeing Toni's face in hers. No words pass between us—she's nonchalantly wiping her face.

"Nothing like a roll of death in the morning, huh?" She mutters unapologetically, with bitterness in her tone, lashing at me. Suddenly my thoughts stream across the many times I heard that before. Even the times when vegan girlfriends forced me to watch cows getting hit with hammers and chickens pecking their legs off.

Knowing what I know, I should really put this sandwich down.

"You look lost in thought." What does she mean by that?

Oh, now she wants to be all arrogant; meanwhile the images of old memories continue to play out in front of my eyes, almost superimposing over her face.

Whew. Finally, I can stop looking at her. Wtf am I so mesmerized?

The cheese is melted all into the Bologna and Mayonnaise. I hate that. "Well, answer my last question." I ask again, as if her attempt to be deflective didn't just take place.

"Yes," her voice now smaller and annoyed.

"Are you registered to vote?"

"Yes." She starts to tap her fingers on my desk.

"Have you filled out your organ donor card?"

"No."

"And have you been tested for Post-Choice Depression?"

"No!" Angrily the words flew out at me.

I don't blame her. This is the part of the job I hate, the part that seems the most racist and elitist.

The question.

The question that targeted the so-called minorities of The Life accusing them of a mental health issue, purportedly originated from that specific group.

Meanwhile any non-minority of The Life, who has the mildest of symptoms, is under-currently considered a victim. Victims.

I mean that's what Directive Living makes them out to be with their city-wide Holo-Ads, I-plant pop-bytes and administering of therapeutic drugs based on demographic research.

And here I am sitting in a cubicle shut off from the world, shoveling that mess into the minds of minorities. *My people. Minorities. Give a me a freakin' break.*

Mafdet keeps staring *into* my face, her eyes sharp, pushing like daggers into my lips every time I speak. But I can't get my mind off that word *minorities,* the one they still use in their legal documents even after all that has happened in the past years. The Renpet Phenomenon developed from local to global proportions, *changing* the genetic codes of thousands … and causing the deaths of tens of thousands.

"Are you sitting there thinking about how much of a scab you are?"

Yes. I really want to say that out loud. But why would I let her know she is right?

Her words somehow caught the tail end of the draft in here making it that much colder, that much lonelier. Difficult to tell if the air grew colder from her words or I was just imagining it.

Tripping. But who could tell what was what these days?
Everything seems out of the ordinary.

"Well?" She's waiting for an answer, growing restless in that big jacket of hers, shifting from side to side in her seat ripping away at a torn patch of leather underneath her.

I'm literally about to let some words leave my lips that would jeopardize my job. *Snap out of it, fall back into protocol. Let your hand discretely slip to the left draw handle. That's it ... same routine. You know this—you got this. Slip out The Confirmation of Attendance papers. You done it many times before to keep your job. Why is this any different?*

Form #1313.

The infamous form that locks the signer into a series of state mandatory home visits and in-person appointments, pressuring them to be monitored and, in my opinion, literally driven to PCD.

Her eyes aren't leaving me.

She's following every move I make—*sooo, make no effort in hiding anything, just slide it in front of her ... to the only place on the desk that has space.*

"Please sign by the x's." The hardest words for me to say each time it comes to this.

What's with her inquisitive yet sarcastic look, like she knows more about this whole process than I do? More about Directive Living than I would ever know. This is weird now. It's not only in her body language. There are these pulses pushing against my skin, coming from her direction. No, they're coming *off* her. A little heat, not aggressive but stern…blue hues of light…

Is that what I am seeing now? They seem to be radiating about her body, moving with the pulses—almost breathing.

"What," she pauses before inching forward in her seat, "makes you think I am signing Constellation 13!?"

Constellation 13. That's what they called this form.

Something to do with a rumor of a thirteenth constellation signaling the end of all things Euro. I never understood what that had to do with the people it affected, since there was no known participation of Euros in the process. Well, I guess for all the non-Euros forced to sign, it meant Directive Living would be in every facet of their lives, so it in some way would be the end. As much as Novus City paints DL in a positive light, there is an overwhelming amount to the contrary that is viral. Just about everything imaginable from Secret Societies to Eugenics to UFOs.

Everything about the rumors is hard to confirm. The only thing I *do* know is this young lady in front of me may not be able to walk out this building if her name is not next to those x's.

"I am not signing it." I can't believe how calmly her small hands crumple up the form.

"Hey Mafdet, I've seen really tough, big guys refuse to sign."

"And?"

"Before they left … they signed."

"Let me put it this way. If my name appears on that paper, in my handwriting …" Her face is getting grim, shifting those pulses.

"… The Devil will kiss God," she answered with a disturbing lack of life in her voice. Another saying of the kids nowadays, usually meant as "fuck off" in a polite way.

What is about to take place next I know very well one-sidedly. I am asked to leave my cubicle while someone comes in to escort my case to my supervisor. Then they are brought back to me a few minutes later, all too eager to sign. And even though they do it with enthusiasm, they still appear to be the same person. It always messes with me, but I never questioned it…openly. No matter how much it tears at my own sensibilities.

I'm hanging onto her last words, doing my best to stall from what I am trained to do next, inches away from reluctantly pressing the worn button underneath my desk.

"Do what you need to do, cause that's what you been *made* to do." Her words stab at all my sensibilities.

My supervisor —whom I've rarely seen—suddenly steps in with two rock-hard looking police officers, bigger than any Handlers I ever seen. "0093139, there are some men here that want to have a word with you."

"Looks like the chickens have come home to roost," Mafdet says slyly.

"You," My supervisor snapped at her, pointing a sharp index finger, "please go down to the reception desk and re-schedule another appointment." His mood lightens as he politely directs her.

Damn!

The officers reach for the side-arms reflexively after I push myself away from my desk, my chair almost hits my supervisor.

Hunching over like this, makes it easier to let the building despair strangle my lungs and take me for a ride. Looking up at the officers, who are getting impatient, and then at my supervisor, who is grinning ear to ear … I am at a loss.

And pulses are coming off them as well…cold…deep red to brown…sickening.

And cold.

Despondence is taking over. All the muscles in my face seem to slide down to my chin and my eyes drying up. I'm beginning to zone out.

"Let's go!" My arm stopped *breathing* when the Officer clamped down on it, at least the pain that came with it kept me present …

With the bullshit.

Chapter 5

CELL

12:30pm

> *How did all this happen?*
> *I thought Toni was halfway sane when we met …in a bar.*
> *Fuck! A boyfriend? For months?*

Four months of no problems. Nothing. A spat here and there about groceries but nothing serious. Oh yeah, there was that time she wanted me—practically begged me— to bring home PCD Suppressants.

> *Funny how that didn't bother me, even when she withheld sex from me.*

But then again, for the whole time we were together she never invited me to her home, or always changed the subject when I brought it up.

Toni had a way of changing minds … but that didn't save her from Wayne. Didn't keep her body from going cold.

Toni.

"Cah-Yakes." Annoying, gurgled and almost greasy the word flies out across from me, shortly followed by the stench of the breath that carried it.

Everything about this place has me wanting to keep still and *be ignored* until I got out of here, whenever that happens. Each time I breathe, it is like cotton being stuffed down my throat.

Something in the air is off. Almost on their own, my eyes are all too eager to focus on one area—the rusted drain in the center of the floor—and dare not wander anywhere else. Regardless of the rustling and shifting of weight on the bench opposite from me, that could potentially be signaling me to start swinging my fists wildly, my vision stays with the corroded steel holes.

Gradually, the awful mixture of what had to be reminiscent of cleaning products used on ragged mops blending into the sweat from the walls, makes the perfect fuming environment to attack my eyes.

Can't take it any longer, forget keeping my eyelids open to be tormented and just plain out rub the shit out them; the cold steel bench creaks out back and forth almost attached to the movements of my hand. Why is a bad scenario flashing before my eyes? Got me pressing my back tight against the wall …

Getting nervous as fuck about drawing too much attention to myself. Uneven, small but sharp edges about the wall poke through the spaces in my sweater, scraping at me.

Need to stop fidgeting about.

If he sees it as a weakness ... takes the opportunity to try to snuff me while I can't see in between the rubbing of my eyes, at least I could spring out at him.

Wonder how my poker-face looks because it feels tight across my face. While blinking the last bit of nastiness out, it forces me to, reluctantly look around at my surroundings—of this dark and damp cell.

With this dude.

I just want to go on vacation.

"Cah-Yaakes." Again, what sounds like *cakes,* echoes eerily throughout the cell.

But this time, a musky body odor is laid into the words, the type of smell of someone that was sweating out PCD-Suppressants and ... soaked in sex.

And it just lingers about within this claustrophobic space of cement block walls and close-knit steel bars, without a window for it to escape. Seemingly feeding off whatever *good* air that did ventilate the space.

Turning it stale ... making me sick.

Not going to answer or turn towards him. Let him keep rambling, mumbling on about strange shit I don't want to hear. Already seen his face when I was first thrown into this cell; the noticeable cuts and marks on it ran deeply into his features and his blank expression.

Even before he winked at me, it wasn't difficult to tell that he was *off*. The way his patchy dark complexion blended into the darkness made the dingy walls behind him seem that much bleaker. The incessant *cah-yakes* don't stop for nothing, with him rocking back and forth on the bench, while the chant bellows from out of the pit of his gut.

Okay, it's getting weird … now he's staring at me as he says it, bloodshot eyes nearly thrusting out their sockets.

Had to piss for the past few minutes, the urge taunting me to get some balls. But the flickering of the lone dim watt bulb above us, and the brown-stained steel toilet right next to him, makes it easy to hold it.

Wait a minute, two COs strolling by, dragging their batons along the bars, my hearing swallowed up into their echoes, makes it difficult to stay on point. My cellmate is taking his eyes off me and whipping his head towards the bars, then back at me with a hard stare abruptly stopping the chanting … silently watching me. My legs are nearly stuck into the floor from fear, but here's an opportunity.

Okay got to get to the toilet as quick as I can, hitting the inside wall— aiming at a fly in a urinal.

"Cah-Yakees!" The sick bastard is rising and starting towards me.

But the two COs charged inside. They came so fast, butt-ends of their batons flying into his abdomen, sending him meekly balled up into the corner.

Damn, I nearly pissed on myself swinging around to look.

One of the COs taps his partner and points at me, laughing his ass off.

Comedy.

Up-Metro Police Stations were pretty ef'd up in comparison to the ones in Down-Metro. I don't know if they have any in Mid-Town. The city made sure to stick the most racist high-ranking officers they could find within these walls. At least that's what it seems like, especially seeing first-hand the amount of Nubian desk officers practically glued to their seats when I walked through the precinct. Along with the Nubian faces behind the bars as I was *escorted* to my cell.

For years community groups, councilmen and major Nubian business owners fought Novus City in the City Hall of Mid-Town, which was about the only time they were allowed on the island and for the most-part off The Bridge.

But nothing changes.

Maybe it was the only way for Novus City to have some sort of foothold in Up-Metro, a way to control the streets—streets that were not backing down.

"A-yo CAKES!" He barks at me like he …

Like he's trying to holla at me.

Not sure if that is the case or not, still need to keep a discreet watch on his body movement. But I am tired of being a pussy. If anything, I am going to strike first.

"Ahem, 0093139."

I didn't want to lift my head up to see who called out my D.L. Id#. *Shit it's my supervisor looking down on me! Wtf is he doing here?*

"Let me in." He turned to the CO with him, tapping the bars, the dull sound of his knuckles going against them brings me nothing but worry.

Did he just stride into the cell, as if it's his own office?

Nudging me over to sit, his polished suit seems to taunt the cah-yakes dude and myself from some high Eurocentric position.

"Listen 0093139 …"

Damn, he's laying a hand on my back—he has me. It just pisses me off to be referred to as a serial number instead of my actual name. *Freakin' corporation protocol.*

"You don't want to be in here for too long." I hate his smirk and the condescending pat on my back while he glances over at the Cah-Yakes Dude. "Not for too long at all. And being involved in … let's say an unfortunate position you are in now," he pauses, and stares at me, taking a hold of my knee shaking it, "it won't keep you employed. Much less *free*."

An ultimatum is coming. His tone changes, and the stagnate air in here shifts. "The Chief of this station is a close acquaintance of mine. And he agrees with me: you were just at the *wrong* place at the wrong time."

I knew it! The rug and her body had my DNA all over them. Had to be. Who needs fluid when they can read skin and heat-crumbs?

"Hey, *Hey!* Stop drifting and pay attention!"

Is he scolding me like I'm a child? If only I wasn't in this position; I'd already be at his throat!

"Now." He pauses then hastily turns away, scrunching up his face. "Remember that case you had right before you ended up in here?"

Turning his head in my direction, the question gingerly leaves his lips. But the quivering of those thin lips afterwards and his flushed pinkish complexion speaks something contrary to his laid-back demeanor.

"Yeah." I feel lifeless.

"We are interested in her … *activities*." His face shifts deviously. "He can go." He points at me and makes some weird gesture with his other hand.

When the guard sees this, he falls back into the bars trying to catch himself. "L-l-let's go you." He stammers nervously, as he slides the gate behind me.

Something about his interaction with my supervisor frightened him. *What could it be? Why is this CO grabbing my shoulder like this? He's trying steer me…no fucks given about my arm about to go dead.*

Cigarette butts, what looked like shit-filled tissues and other nasty things came flying from out between the bars quickly filling up the path I walked.

"Scab!"

One screams out followed by another. "Euro bitch!"

From just about every dark cell comes insults and threats. Did they somehow know what took place in my cell or could it be something else?

"Cah-Yakes! D-d-don't let them make you eat them *ca-cakes!*" My former cellmate's words were loud and clear, there was no mistaking them.

Don't eat them cakes.

Something was being placed in their food.

"Move it!" The guard's fingers are pressing even harder into my shoulders as he pushes me forward. "I don't know *who* you are, but I don't want to be around you for too long. *C'mon!*"

"Why?" *Shit, why I let that slip out? Why? It could be interpreted as anything and I just said it from feeling hopeless.* "Tell me why?" again, I plead.

What am I doing? Why am I asking this guy anything? That's risking a club across the back of the head—or worse.

"You really want to know?" His whisper into my ear as he passes by me is nothing less than unsettling.

Maybe it'll be nothing. I mean we are still walking the same direction I came in after being booked, so that means on the way out of here. Wait. He's turning to me face to face. Cat looks like something straight out one of those grimy police dramas.

Didn't really get a whiff of the odd funk coming of his body because he was behind me.

But now I do.

"Okay, I'll tell you. But first we need to get somewhere private."

Oh shit, I just possibly set something off I can't deal with.

Slowly we seem to be deviating from the path—the white lines on the floor are gradually changing from white to red. Cat has me creeping under and pass cameras embedded in walls, windows of dark offices and in some areas of the floor itself. This has me even more worried than I already am—who's going to let someone go that knows police security systems?

The usual background sounds you would hear in a precinct; from walking through doors, footsteps, talking or moving papers is vanishing. Neck's getting stiff from keeping my head up, so I'll just let it drop— no more lines on the floor—just worn away black and white tile.

"Awannaknow in 5." What is he talking about to someone on his receiver?

"What was all that about?" Again, I risk a swift and painful response asking questions.

"Nothing to be concerned with. Just how we keep all this on the hush."

Did he just pity-pat me on the back before hitting a button on his utility belt? The cuffs snap open.

My wrists can breathe again. Guess he's not worried about me running off.

Strange thing though, they don't fall, just rest on my wrists, kind of want to go with that image running through my mind …

Of me breaking them across his jaw. But I won't be doing that.

Crap my neck hurts—the cuffs are already removed, but I barely notice him doing it. Coming to a narrow stairwell; I'm sure to trip down its winding darkened path. It's getting hard to breathe, the air almost feels toxic.

I start coughing.

"Quit all the coughing and shit," his raspy whisper literally feeds into the short jab in the gut from the baton. It doesn't hurt…

Much.

We are at the bottom; chills are coming over me.

I am in trouble.

"C'mon, we're here."

The door is dusty as hell. It probably hasn't been opened for months, and as he creaks it open foul ranking smells fly out.

"In *here?*" It's hard to hide the fear in my voice. Doing my best not to crap in my pants.

Why did I even want to know?

My eyes!

Okay, I can see again … Why he flicked the lights on like that?

Before the struggling lightbulbs could stop rattling, I am getting pushed in. He steers me along by my neck. My eyes can't help but to dart about the room, got to keep my head in one position without being noticed. Straining my eyes from the lack of light and trying to see areas beyond my peripheral could be why I am getting a migraine right now.

I'm all sorts of fucked up right now.

I ignore the strain until I finish going over all the areas of the room more than once. Looks like a morgue that was shut down some time ago. I can only make out shadowy outlines of steel gurneys pushed up to the sides and boxes of files scattered about.

"My friends will be here soon—they'll tell you everything you want to know."

I'm sorry Toni, coldly, but silently, her name slips from my lips, as if she's somewhere alive on my breath.

I clutch at my chest to stop her name from heaving out again. It doesn't work, and my tears can't be held back. It's hard to stand…

Finding myself on my knees.

"Look at this guy."

I barely heard the new voice in the room, even though its booming above me—I feel weightless. For some reason, my childhood memories are bubbling up…crawling over my skin with images.

"Blubbering over your little girlfriend, huh?"

What he said stung, crowded up my head, triggering years of self-pity wanting release. But its short lived, killed-off by the sharp-point of a long shoe shot into my stomach.

"*Argggh!*" I can't hold it in.

"Shut up Nub! You better hold that shit in, or this can get much worse for you!" By his gruff voice I know he means every word of it.

The shoe nearly cut into my insides. *I don't care … Maybe I deserve it.*

But the lingering smell of Anti-RP creme intermingled with sweat is too much to ignore—enough to jog me out my neurosis. These four dudes circling around me, more than likely are addicted to it— Anti-RP creme never completely protected the skin from sunburn anyway; it just caused the skin to release more oil.

It's fucked up.

I even heard that some users suffer from a kind of 'roid rage, nothing a citizen would want to see in their police force.

What *is* that?

Toni?

From out of thin air her face slowly streams together in an electrical purplish mist—ghostly, breaking apart and reforming as before. Transparent, almost vaporous, but I *know* it's her.

"You want to know what all this is about, Nub?"

Raspy tones mix in with aggression, grating into his voice. The sound of it gets my stomach in a knot.

I can't get out the way quick enough to avoid his hand swiftly diving through Toni's face. He's got a grip on a tuft of my hair pulling my head up. The smile across his face, while he slowly kneels to me shows how much he is getting off on all of this.

"This is all about something special about … your people. Something you are all born with."

Some small flecks of dead skin fly into my eye every time he speaks—along with spittle.

This guy is literally falling apart. Wait—don't let my hair go! I can't stop my face from smashing into the floor. *Arrgh…it hurts!*

Crepitus rings out from his knees as he clumsily springs up. For a moment it takes me away from the throbbing in my face. But I need to see what's going. I can turn my head to one side, that's about all. Never heard anyone grunt the way he did before shaking his legs out.

Good ... he's walking towards the others. My nose is leaking, just noticed the drops in front of me. Whatever that special thing was, it isn't going to be found out today.

Or any other. They aren't going to leave me alive.

"Dillon, your turn to take one in the leg."

"Already?" The reluctance in his voice sends chills up my spine, while the unmistakable sound of a pistol being cocked back echoes through the room.

I can't stop shaking—footsteps coming toward me. Need to fight back ...barely feel my arms and legs.

"Well Nub, anything you want to say."

There's a lot I'd like to say but what's the use?

"Brrrrr, did you guys feel that draft?" the dismay in his voice shifts everything.

I may just survive this.

"What the *fuck* is it?"

"The *lights*—!"

The bulbs literally *crack,* and the room goes dark, pitch. Its growing cold—the floor is sapping heat from my body.

"Where's the *switch?* Find the freakin' light switch!" one of them yells hoarsely.

"There's one by the door … let me get my cell phone out to se—"

"Way ahead of you, pulled out my cell as soon as the lights went out, doesn't work. No power."

"Anyone upgraded their I-plants?"

At this point it's hard to distinguish who is who; they're all going up and down in their tones.

"Who can afford *that?*"

They trip about, hesitant in their steps. They forget about me. And all these *What the hell to do next?* scenarios I'm coming up with require energy.

Energy I don't have.

"*Erk*" one of them gasps.

"Dillon?" Nervously slips from another.

Dillon, that's the one who was going to take one for the team. Sounds like he just did.

Shit! What's going on?

"Warren is that you touching me?" Another one stammers.

"Get outta the room, George!"

"Something else is in here with us—run!" They can barely talk.

Got just about all their names. *But so what?*

All their footsteps are getting slower, less stumbling and no talking— just the type of movement when people sneak around.

Something else *is* in the room with us. Its *steps* vibrate lightly across my belly through the floor as it moves about.

"*Arrgh!*" one of them is howling, his scream joined by something breaking, then snapping.

This can't be happening.

Against the backdrop of the yelling, I can barely make out someone gurgling, choking … a strange faint grinding sound of bone against bone follows. With all this craziness taking place, my heart is thumping so hard my whole body's rocking up and down against the floor. And I am getting colder. Without heat, I can't produce energy to get up out of here.

"*Noooooo …!*" a shout, that becomes a wheeze, fills the entire room.

Wtf? That's a sound I'm unfamiliar with.

"My arm … my *arm* … its … it's *being* …!" The scream is unreal.

Each time something happens I can't help but to cringe and brace to be hit or worse.

What a bitch I am.

Well, at least I am getting a bit of heat now. Can barely keep myself from losing it though. Loud *crack* after crack keeps snapping out into the darkness…with little cracklings breaking off after it.

The screaming has stopped … feeling weak … Oh no not ag—

These blaring lights are burning into my eyes. Why did I even flick my lids open? Everything is fuzzy.

Lost consciousness.

Good, the ceiling is slowly coming into focus. *Someone got me onto my back.* Even though there is a chill still running about the room, it's not like it was earlier. But then again, all my limbs are numb. Can't hold my head up properly; it hurts drooping over like this. Maybe I ca—

Tubes are sticking out of my arm!

What the hell are tubes doing sticking out of my arm? Is this all I can do? Lay here unable to move, staring at the almost luminescent liquid running through the tubes into my body. More of the room is coming into focus. I'm able to follow the tubes back to … a machine?

I'm strapped to a gurney! "WHAT THE FUCK IS GOING ON HERE?" Yelling is only making my throat sore, only to be met with my voice echoing back at me with a steely feel off the walls.

The pressure in the tubes is changing—another dosage of drugs…ahhh…I'm starting to care about none of this.

Okay…okay all those echoes are settling down; managing to still care about something without aggravating this drug-induced euphoria allowing me to float above it all. One of the figures from out the right corner is approaching me.

"Keep your voice down 93139." That's my supervisor's voice. Uh…yea, now I can see him boldly leaning up against the straps and railing, crouching over to look down on me: emotionless. "Lucky for you we came in when we did."

"Why? Why am I all plugged up?" *Throat hurts so much to talk. This is a nightmare.*

"Never seen anything like it. You?" One EMS worker says to the other holding the other end of a stretcher, a long black bag limply rocks along on it—that much I can see.

"W-w-what happened?"

"We should be asking *you* that. And why whatever madman that came through here left you *alive*."

I hear the words but can't help but feel unattached to them. "What?" I *been* had enough, so keeping my professionalism is the last thing on my mind.

Where were the COs?

"Keep calm."

Wait a minute. Who told you, you could place your hand on my chest? The coldness of it went right through my clothing; the pounding of my heart practically jumps into his palm.

Can't focus. Everything in me wants to get out.

"He's going into arrest!" My supervisor abruptly calls to one of the others in the room.

This is not good.

"His MSH levels are almost off the chart!"

"Even with the inhibitors we introduced—they are literally encouraging the surrounding melanocytes to eat through them!"

"No…it seems the white blood cells are being directed by his neuromelanin to *target* the proteins of the inhibitors like they were viral infection."

"Astounding!"

I don't fully understand what they're getting at, but I get enough for me to really panic. The monitors practically scrape at my eardrums going off crazily in response.

I'm slippi …

"Keep him alive! We need more samp—"

Today is just not my day. Most of it has been spent passing out. How much time have I lost? And this time they moved me from the station—back to a DL med unit and put me in a gown. At least I'm not bound to anything or stabbed up with Ivies, but my chest feels strange.

Sore.

So reluctant to reach under my gown and lightly sweep my fingers over *bandages?* Bandages and something weird underneath …

Staples!

I can't hit the nurse button enough, getting drained by the thought of what they may tell me when they come in.

"We had to do a heart transplant," my supervisor says a little too evenly, stepping out from the shadows.

Wait a minute what the fu— "Y-y-you *what?*" *It* can't *be. Nothing is wrong with me. My heart is just fine. Nothing is wrong with it.*

"There, there now. Our specialist is the best." The words that calmly come out his mouth echo the elitism of Mass Gentrification.

"There, *there* now? What do you mean? *You had no right!*" I can barely raise up to drop this fuckbag—stinging in my chest…can't stop from falling back into the bed. My entire world has just collapsed into shit. My eyes are stinging, begging to well up…but I won't let them.

"We are repairing your heart." His voice and demeanor carry no life.

Wait a minute…what did this mofo just say? Repair? DL doesn't have that ability on their premises.

"Meanwhile we have fitted you with a prosthetic one designed by one of our sister companies."

"I can't believe this … I want my heart back *now.*" No strength to reach up to him; my arm keeps feebly dropping back down against the railing.

His quivering chest rises and falls.

Like he really cares.

"Of course, and this brings us to the matter of the meeting that will take place this evening."

He can't be serious.

"The stakes are obviously a bit higher now. It's an expensive procedure to repair your heart, something your health insurance doesn't cover. Barely covered the one we performed."

Smug bastard. He knows that if my new pay grade was approved earlier this year, by him, *that any procedure would be covered by Directive Living.*

"We will have your heart fully repaired within a few hours, luckily that implant will hold up just long enough." He speaks so directly, like he is referring to a piece of property. "Give him whatever you need to give him to get him out this bed and ready to work," he barks to a group of people in lab coats tentatively huddled up by a gurney on the other side of the room.

I am screwed.

3:30pm

Chapter 6

MEETING

7:00pm

"So, let me get this *straight, ah-right.*" Some of the attendees around him giggle when the words *straight* tauntingly left his lips. His flamboyant gesturing isn't helping either.

"You want to take us all to another country?" He pauses to purse his lips. "A country only for us?" His hand on his hip is now more dramatic handplay.

The small conversations buzzing about since we started our meeting simmered down when that last word left his mouth. The hush of their lips, whose air pressure I *feel* unintentionally, sweeps briskly through the rows and aisles followed by a deep and almost annoying silence…

Something about it is very unsettling to me. What are these cold sensations shooting through me, and the shaking, I am unable to control or…mask easily? As much as I want to, I can't keep my eyes from swiftly running over the many faces in the audience then towards the cold, uninviting concrete walls of the school's auditorium. All the while, secretively wishing that we had our usual conference room at the hotel on the Upper-Eastside instead.

I could really use all its warmth and hospitality right about now. It's difficult to muster my strength back up to speak.

"Sit…you have done enough tonight."

What's with Josie pushing me down into the chair despite the obvious protests of my body locking in place.

"I'm fine." Shooing her away nearly exhausts me. "Don't let them see me needing help. I'm fine." My light whisper barely catches her attention.

Doing my best to hide the bits of grunts of pain that slip through my lips—can barely manage to lean up against the podium and remain conscious. C'mon Mafdet, stop fumbling through your papers…and thoughts.

Unconsciously exchanging glances with that annoying guy who asked that question … More spells of dizziness coming on. My neck is getting all sweaty, too quick for me to be comfortable with.

"Well?" He stands with his arms folded tightly over his chest and smirks at me, but his jerking body language shows he is unsure or feeling defensive.

He turns to look down with a smile at his little peanut gallery in the seats next to him. The audience responds like they are watching a tennis match, and I was just served. Their heads spin in unison, the gathered thoughts come crashing over me like a wave.

Thanks, Josie, for easing up beside me and clutching my hand; it breaks my connection with the emotional wind.

"Go on…" she urged. Her words are a comfort.

I want her hand to stay with mine, ground me so I am not swept up by all these sensations—but she pulled away.

Too late.

Things are becoming blurry, the crowd unrecognizable. My senses are being dragged into their accumulated pocket of emotions and memories of my own. I cannot sense my body…

Or myself.

Although numbness travels throughout my body, every part of it is reliving the memories of the first time the vision struck me. *The first time I pulled.*

Can it really be called that? It can't be a vision when your whole body gets physically hauled somewhere you never seen before. A place you can't put into words. Nothing prepared me to handle the responsibility of it all…*at all.*

But Josie after a detailed agonizingly long-winded descriptive conversation felt it was what people in The Life were looking for.

She went on and on about how it would benefit people from all over the world. I remember how bright her eyes were and how her voice was filled with enthusiasm. That was until I told her it did not include *all* people in The Life—only those of a dark hue. Nubians. After that she tussled with her own cultural identity, having a father of near pure, as she liked to say, German Stock and a mother of Kenyan origin.

This can't be happening right now.

It almost unbelievable how I am living that whole experience in such a short amount of time—in front of all these people. Pulled into the days when our conversation was limited, even at breakfast, during the time we would watch the O channel for new trends in fashion and such.

Disturbingly quiet.

Until the first day of fashion week premiered on O…

"You need to share this with others," she abruptly broke days of silence, a mouthful of cereal gurgling her words, "and with people who can make it happen." The enthusiasm she had when I first told her returned.

Remembering all of it. Feeling all of it too well.

"Let's do meet-ups." She pulled out her laptop and began a search and that's how a small meet-up turned into weekly meetings like this one …

And that's how I slowly became a mess.

Oh great, the vision stopped. Okay now back to this fool.

"Yes, it will be a country of sorts. Where we will be amongst our own…only."

The answer leaves my lips with such conviction, that it takes him by surprise.

And when did I get back to the podium?

The challenging look, along with the sass that filled his face, drops from it as he quietly eases back into his seat.

What a relief. I really don't like conflict.

Slowly my stomach is settling or at least going back to its normal queasiness. The expecting faces, who only moments ago drove their skepticism at this podium and me, lost much of their angst. But what is building in place of it, is the same indescribable feeling I experienced at prior meetings.

Except now it slams against my being.

It's never quite a smell, sound, or any of the other things my senses pick up. Something beyond all those things calls me … beckons my spirit. Pulling at my ribcage then tugging at my heart. And it only came from being around even just one person in The Life…

One Nubian person.

What I can't put into words, literally swims off their bodies in waves of energy. Maybe it came from their spirits and minds as well, who knew?

And it was stronger when the more of us gathered.

"Maffie …" Is that Josie's whispering, faintly coming from my side, pulling me back to the present? "Stay here." Her whisper comes again, this time with worry. The worry in her voice only means one thing. "Breathe slower, Maffie."

Yes, Josie talk to me. I don't know what to do. Guide me.

I could hardly get my chest to rise and fall evenly in those last few breaths, but the sensation of pulling from the audience is easing up…something that I had been doing unconsciously for the last thirty minutes. Parts of me are finally beginning to close, the pores of my skin tightening, my hearing withdrawing and my sense of touch returning to back to me.

Also, I have stopped taking from everyone in the room, the one thing that was unknown to me.

But I knew was there.

And with it, *I, myself,* cease to be pulled towards an opening—that I made on my own. What would the crowd say if they could see this pinhole into the cosmos lying in the middle of my papers? Energy pulsating about in a thickness of dark space. My face must be flushed because of the chills running through it. Thank goodness for my next to ebony skin. This next wave coming over my cheeks, is almost blending evenly with this sensation I can't shake. I can't tell whether I am projecting onto myself or not, but the eyes I contact, in the audience, are sending something back to mine.

Eyes reflecting exactly what was being done to them.

And as usual (as with other meetups), they seem aroused by what I did to them, slowly gyrating their bodies and subtly touching themselves within the aisles before me.

The opening is closed.

Whatever the thing I was doing has completely stopped. Some participants are looking around in embarrassment, others asking their neighbor, "Did you just feel that?"

And some are staring at me…just staring.

"Okay everyone our little friend here is drained, too much excitement for one night." Josie gently pushes me aside to take the podium.

I *am* so drained.

Wobbling over to the chair that she had offered me earlier on and doing my best, since eyes were still on me, not to completely collapse in it is a task.

"We are taking a little break. There are refreshments in the back." Josie politely tells the audience, hiding her own anxiety.

While slouching in this chair is my trending thing to do, along with thinking of ways to stay awake, I can't help but hope that the correct food was ordered: a light vegan buffet. These people don't need the heaviness of the fast food, meat, and dairy.

Especially if they decide to go where I want—no am being guided *to take them.*

"We got more donations and pledges in our account!" Josie gleefully holds up her I-phone and does a little dance, bringing me some sense of relief.

Guess she *should* be happy, rent's due, and it's been a little slow at the fabric store in the garment district. Sometimes it feels like she gets all caught up in the money a little too much. The money is to fuel the mission, not our pockets. Josie may not be coming with us.

Or me.

Any who with most of the participants focusing on eating and each other, I can finally relax and let myself completely sink into this uncomfortable chair.

This metal back is pushing into me like it has some personal issues with me. But exhaustion has an interesting way of making anything tolerable and then comfortable. Funny how the more I let go of being mad at it, the more the backrest becomes pillow soft.

And now, drifting off is becoming more and more of what I want to do, my body practically melting into every part meeting it … regardless of all the voices chattering about in the background. Voices and tones sliding into one another, liquid into vapor becoming electricity.

I want to go home.

"Drink."

Why is Josie pushing a cup of some red juice in my face? "Does it have any dyes in it? It looks a little strange." My limbs are getting weak, sleep is coming. *How groggy I must look to her.*

"Maybe," she mutters softly.

But she's pissing me off. Why? "Give me water—give me water now!"

Something is taking a hold of me. A surge of uncontrollable distaste for anything impure flooding my senses. Sweeping through them. Why is she passing me a plastic bottle of water, as if she doesn't know any better?

Why didn't she just give it to me in a glass bottle? "Josie, where's my glass bottle?" I snap at her. I couldn't help myself; the small contact I make with the plastic irritates my skin.

"Sorry heifer, I forgot."

The sincerity in her voice means nothing. I don't care for her apology because she *knows* I have removed food colorings, preservatives, and syrups, amongst other contaminates from my eating. Ever since that day I received the first vision, eating junk-food or anything processed for that matter, makes my body weak…sick.

Being pulled into that place, that world, my body has never been the same. The forces there turned my cells inside out, stripped them clean then filled with …

Light, at least that is what it felt like.

Josie knows nothing about how I been feeling. I never told her in full detail, but I think she is getting the picture that something is off … given that we have been less sexually active.

I can't stop my eyes from wandering over to the plastic bottle sitting up on the podium. I'm just noticing Josie's eyes fixed on me…intensely.

Can she read my mind? I didn't know that!

"Yes, I can," her whisper isn't encouraging.

"You *what?*" *Crap, I yell that out* loud, *turning the heads of the attendees at the buffet.*

People in The Life love a bit a drama and I can't see any of them passing up some free entertainment, so I better cool down. Josie's not changing her position though. Her face is plastered with seriousness, her glare digging into me.

"I see."

She's responding to my thoughts. This can't be! Is it happening to her as well? Don't think anything else; she'll see into things I'm still sorting out … hiding.

"Yup, it cannot be helped—that you are so gullible," blurting out teasingly like that was her way of easing tension.

But just to continue laughing, slapping your leg, and jumping up holding your stomach, is a little much.

"HaHaHa*cough**cough*HaHaHa…you*cough**cough* are so…"

Josie's not quite getting the words out. Maybe choking will bring her back. Why did I start thinking in that direction? My mind is beginning to wrap around the idea that she will soon be gone from my life.

"Drink the juice I gave you in the first place."

Oh, she's being so demanding!

"It's just pomegranate. Damn!" Her voice and all its attitude seem to reach out for the ears of all them folk in the back.

Oh, *now* that you see them facing us, some starting to lean up against the table, sipping on their cups and eyeballing us, your tone wants to calm down. Wish it were that easy for me though. Thoughts swimming chaotically, bumping into the small amount of peace I managed to build up from earlier.

"Josie, stop looking at me." She caught me sniffing around for anything artificially added, before tilting the spout over my lips.

It's okay. It's refreshing to say the least and as it runs through my insides.

I feel a bit ashamed for checking the contents, carrying on without any trust in Josie. Well, not Josie, but the drink itself.

What can anybody trust as being naturally grown anyway? Ever since we entered the phenomenon the world is calling *Renpet,* The Great Year, companies have rushed to practically patent words like agave and natural, and … *organic.*

Farms have converted to locally fresh supermarkets on demand delivery. You can basically walk in and buy freshly grown animals—of course you need to have the right paperwork. Some seniors in the park say they used to be run by farming families and owned privately by them. That was too much to take. Too much to think about and rationalize to be able to eat properly.

Guess that's how my OCD was born. A habit that came about out of fear of not knowing what my biology was like anymore.

I don't know what it is now, but it's nothing close to what it was before the first Bridge swallowed me. *Bridges.* Josie couldn't have chosen a better name for it.

"Excuse me," a voice is calling out to me, dragging me out of my daydream.

"Mafdet!" Whoa, my head sprung up quicker than my senses could follow. No wonder that looking right at a person doesn't register anything. *"Mafdet!"* The young man in front of me is talking, but it's like everything he's saying is muffled.

"Josie, what the hell? Is she having another one of her spells?" This time when he spoke, a name came to the surface through the muddiness.

"Ray." I know him. "R-Ray I apologize…" Ray has been a bestie of ours for years, one of the only people we knew who has an apartment in Up-Metro.

"Used to it." His voice…is even less attached than his words.

Uh-Oh. That can be an issue; usually when he sounds that way it can only mean he's up to something.

"Got someone I want you to meet."

How come I didn't see this guy next to him this whole time? Some big dude. He seems dangerous. He doesn't look right. Something in his energy is off. Wait a minute ... it's the guy from the train earlier!

"My name is Wayne."

The heaviness of his voice makes my skin crawl, and the hesitation in it disturbs my spirit. *I don't want to talk to him. Please don't make me even have to look at him any longer.*

Why is Josie's elbow nudging the mess out me? Her eyes are literally telling me to stop being rude. Doesn't she recognize him from the train? Why can't I speak up for myself?

"Nice to meet you Wayne." That felt nasty, forcing the words out my mouth against my better judgement. But I am *not* going to shake his hand.

"My name is Mafdet." That *strange* look from him is less appealing than him trying to sound out my name with his lips. *Oh no. He put his hand out.*

Something is going to happen if we touched, I know it.

Reluctantly, my hand moves meekly towards his. And I swear to all this inner dialogue I am not doing it. I'm almost close enough to touch his hand.

What a minute...are things really beginning to move slow down or am I moving fast? The air around me is becoming thick, pushing against me....and everyone around me is moving ...sluggishly. And my hand—what's with my hand? I can't pull it back!

Looking at Ray in this space of movement, I can see how he has always had bad intentions. Nothing is escaping my perception.

Things are opening and clearly showing themselves.

It's strange to see the muscles around his eyes gradually fold into menacing shapes, raising his eyebrows to continue that path … and his eyes catching a gleam of light.

Chaos.

And wow! Right after that, negative pulses of energy — because they are not moving naturally—wave out from head. This is why he's one *bestie* I could do without. His friendship was one that was forced—since he was there when I accidently opened my first Bridge. And he openly admitted, on that day, that if there was ever a break in friendship on that day, there would be a break in trust.

"Is there something wrong?" Ray says.

Funny how things speed back up after Ray speaks, and fakes being polite, while vapors of frustration leave his pores.

The energy placed in me by that other world…is starting to awaken.

"Ray its fine; she's just a little shy that's all." Wayne's offer of assistance seems very uncharacteristic with all that madness steaming off *his* body.

Geez, another something else is starting to pulse thickly around him, mixing into the air, becoming visible … a murky cloud. Ray is determined, thinking I don't see him grabbing Wayne's hand just before *he* pulls back.

"Ray! *No!*" Josie freaks me out, screaming like that. She falls to her knees and curls up in fetal position.

She knows what is about to happen.

"Oh my God! Oh my God! Not again—not *again!*" Josie is hysterically shaking her head from side to side, eyes squeezed tightly shut.

And me unable to move from this spot …

Getting weak, no strength to pull away from Ray…and almost not caring at this point.

"I want this." Ray's words carry a voice that is not his own. Our hands, Wayne's and my own, are lightly touching, only by the fingertips…the space in front of us is tearing open….

A bridge…

Chapter 7

Everything from This Point on Will...

9:00pm

What happened? Hell, I'm doing on the floor? Why is my head pounding? What is happening to me? Clothes drenched in sweat and my mouth dry as shit ... Was I dreaming?

Nah—my hand slipping in spit while trying to push myself up is not dreaming. Can barely roll over, which is about all I can do.

Ray is next to me knocked out. Wipe this spit on his pants leg. *Fuck*, smearing it into his pants caused his body to shift to turn to face me, drooling and snoring his ass off ... but smiling.

How did I ever get mixed up with my cousin like this? *Oh yeah ... he paid me and said he would help me with my recent blackouts. Like he always says he will.*

It's crazy how all the other lames, who were just drinking and talking their asses off a little while ago, are laid out all over the place. Some slouched over each other, others slumped over chairs—everywhere. Hard to see anything up in here, all the lights even the emergency ones are shut-off. Usually, those lights come on when the main ones lose power, at least they do in Complex D.

Some of the streetlights must be out too, there is barely *any* light coming in through the windows.

Shit...what happened here?

I-plant not responding. Wait a minute. My cell. Its fully charged, but it's in Ray's pocket. Never gave it back after he was finished *borrowing it*. Could his pants be any tighter?

Bruh! Could hardly get it out of his pocket. Freakin' skinny jeans.

Good...screen finally finished with the routine upgrade mess *no one* pays attention to. Damn, not one bar for reception. He's groaning...so caught up with the phone I forgot about Ray.

Him moving around shows he's not dead or anything. But all that murmuring in his sleep, like he was disturbed by something in a dream, won't stop me from fucking him up when he wakes.

Something tells me this is all his fault.

Anyone else would have already woke him up and barked on him for whatever they thought he did, and he did do *something*. Not me though. This time, right now in this auditorium filled with all these passed out people, is like the only time I have a moment to myself...something I haven't had in a long time.

No drama.

Even the throbbing headache shaking the crap out the inside of my head, is more welcome than dealing with someone or anyone *at this moment.*

Thirsty…need something to drink…about to pass out.

I didn't think I was weak, but I must be since I stumbled to my feet. *Arm's getting tired; it's hard to keep this cell light beaming ahead of me, especially with my feet bumping into people's bodies along the way.*

It's not pitch black but shit its close enough. Even with my cell's backlight, my eyes are having a hard time making anything out. Anyone else may go ape shit with all this pushing, just about kicking bodies to the side, trampling on others to get into the aisle.

Not me.

To do what I *must*, I can ignore my foot mashing down on something soft then hard, like someone's fingers.

Must stay focus and not get emotional. Don't need to blackout again…and forget everything I did.

Or get the **I-PLANT EMO-SENSORS,** all about this auditorium next to the cameras, to not only notify the authorities but Complex D as well. Cause' you know not only is the city all in your affairs, so is your place of work. Glad I had my homie *alter* the sensitivity within my I-plant…*hopefully he really did it.*

Can barely walk, stay getting weaker in my legs, but need to keep on. Again, my foot hitting someth—someone's neck! Arrgh…trying to stop my momentum got my legs buckling underneath me.

That's crazy how the cell just flew out my hand and tumbled over a couple of bodies, its light beaming across faces and arms of people before stopping to face the Buffet Table …

Need to eat.

K. Get back up…keep it pushin.'

Alright at the table, took long enough to get here but screw it I am here. Hmmm…this thing looks like a bottle, can't be choosy and shit right now… crap my teeth!

Dummy these things have caps.

Great, it took my last bit of strength to get the cap off only to have half of the juice on my shirt 'cause I forgot how to drink properly. At least the few gulps of about the best juice I ever drank, got me not wanting to pass out anymore.

K. Need to make my way *back* through the littered path of bodies to Ray—wait a minute, something stinging in my head…images…things blocked in my memory.

AHHHHH!

The lights sprung back on like the Sun just popped out of nowhere. And just like that, people are starting to stretch and yawn.

The same ones that looked lifeless earlier.

Most seem confused and shocked to hell to wake up with their face pressed against the school floor, the ledge of chairs, in someone's lap or mashed up in a plate full of food.

I need to quickly get back over to Ray. The surprised looks on their faces, seem to be moving into expressions of anger. Small groups coming together discussing what could have happened, then pulling into larger groups. Becoming a tightly packed mob heading over for that girl Mafdet.

Shit is about to jump off.

"Maffie! *Maffie!*" Her friend is screaming out desperately, rocking back and forth on the floor with Mafdet in her lap.

Mafdet's trembling, her legs kicking and scraping along the floor. Looks like she is having some sort of attack. Should I do anything about it? Considering that crazy shit that took place earlier…should I even be near her?

Who is that whizzing past me and rushed to Mafdet's side? He looks like he doesn't know what to do—whipping his head around in every direction —finally stopping and looking down at Mafdet. What the hell did he just do? Why is prying open her mouth and shoving his hand in like a karate chop?

What the fuck is going on?

***

My fingers are practically numb against her teeth, digging into them with no remorse, getting weird sensations as her tongue laps against them while I tried to hold it down. Empathy is fighting a battle against the drugs DL shot into my body. Mafdet's eyes are rolling around erratically and her huffing out her nose into my face should issue more of a response from me.

Poor child.

This wasn't well thought out at all, but I couldn't stand by idly like all the people who crowded in around her. Some of these bastards are digging frantically in their pockets for their phones, and multiple sent im' notifications are chiming out one after another. Some are just watching intensely, probably recording everything in their I-plants. Others toggle between struggling to look then turning away disturbed, only to look again but do nothing.

It just dawned on me, with all this confusion, why haven't the **EMO-SENSORS** been triggered? And I am sure the cameras in here have caught just about everything that took place…

That we didn't see.

"Try to relax Mafdet. Breathe slowly through your nose. Calm down." The words that leave my lips are barely convincingly. I can't imagine how my cracked voice could offer any comfort…along with my hand shoved in her mouth.

Arrrghhh! Damn that hurt a little, even with the Euphoric moods swinging back and forth through my body.

Crying out on the inside of my head completely wiped away the memory that just popped up on what to do in situations like these. But I did know that shoving my hand in her mouth was not the correct protocol.

None of this is going to help me get out of Novus City for that vacation.

This is not what DL will call "observing the situation quietly." And to make matters worse, when I rushed to Mafdet's aid, Wayne's face swept by my eyes in a blur. Well at least, he's only standing there and watching without changing his position.

"Are you Josie?" She's barely noticing that I'm shaking her arm; she's still holding Mafdet's head in place on her lap. "Listen to me …" My words aren't reaching her; she just keeps shaking her head, while her tears fall to Mafdet's face. "Josie, Josie!" Let me try placing my hand lightly on her cheek, that might snap her out of it.

"What —*what?*" She's back to the present but not without pulling Mafdet's head along when she moved, painfully yanking at my fingers.

"Try to relax. She is almost through it now."

Little by little Josie's breathing grows calmer, as she rubs at her eyes and sniffles.

"Who are you?" She's looking at me funny—at my hand jammed in her girlfriend's mouth.

What am I going to say to her? She caught me off guard. Scenario after scenario runs through my head…an answer's creeping to the surface.

"A friend." *That's all she needs to know for now.* "A friend that wants his hand back." I'm forcing a smirk, now worried more than ever about what all this will mean in the end.

Gently, pressure eases its way down off my hand. At last *freedom*. All that kicking and jerking about, that shook Josie and myself, came to an abrupt stop. Mafdet's is breathing normally, and so am I.

Faint sighs of relief slip out from different parts of the crowd. *They ain't do shit, so I don't see why.*

Cautiously, as slow as possible, I pull my hand from out her mouth, unsticking flesh from her teeth.

"You okay?" Josie muttered to me, but I am too busy stuck on how deep the teeth marks are dug into my fingers, and how no skin was broken.

"Yeah." I guess I am …for the moment.

With a murderer, whose act I eye-witnessed, baring down on me, how should I be? Oh yeah, and with a prosthetic heart in my chest and a crap load of drugs swimming around my system.

No cap. Just don't look up at him. Stay here … be with Josie and Mafdet. He probably doesn't know anyway. How could he?

But something in me keeps ignoring the rational thought that keeps screaming out, *It's okay!* My heart's quickening in pace as I try to stop my head from rising towards Wayne.

My eyes find his. *You killed her.*

It was like the words poured out from my eyes and into his. And no matter how much I want to turn away, the truth and my eyes seem intent on letting him know I *knew*.

You fucking murderer. Now it feels, beyond my control, my entire face is yelling at him, my tongue moving in my mouth with every word in my head. Part of me wants to pounce on him and choke his life out from his throat.

But Wayne is looking blandly back at me. He doesn't pick-up on *anything*. In fact, he turns to some dude next to him and starts arguing.

"Mister …" Josie's calling out to me, but I barely hear her.

"Bruh." She's tugging at my sleeve.

"Yes?" Answering her, made it easier to look away from Wayne and the rage that's building.

"How do you know Maffi—Mafdet?" Everything about her that was polite before. Now she's pushy.

I need to just walk off without answering. Mafdet is still unconscious.

"I asked you a question." Her voice is getting turnt up. Ignore what is quickly becoming an interrogation. Stand-up and walk away; leave Josie and Mafdet on the floor. Something is stirring in me, as I make my way through the crowd, almost pulling me to turn around and go back.

"Hey, you know what happened to us?" Someone blurts out to me. They don't have to lay a hand on my chest like that.

"No." She's making me kinda nervous. I brush off her hand, anxious just to get out of here.

I've seen all that I needed to see … a little too much. *Mysteriously passing out after her speech and now remembering bits and pieces … of things that can't be real, pushing me even further to leave as soon as possible.*

"*He* doesn't know anything—buut that Josie girl should know!" another speaks out.

"What the fuck did you *do* to us?" someone else screams shaking their fist.

"How come I feel sick to my stomach and can hardly breathe?" A girl falls to her knees, almost sobbing. "You a psychic witch or something like that?"

When she blurts this question, you could hear a pin bounce off the ground.

"She must be one!"

"Yeah, that's why she always sick at every meeting and shit!"

Amidst all this building tension, all *I* need to do is keep walking, keep my back turned to the madness brewing behind me …

Almost to the exit.

"Fuck all of *you!*" A loud voice roars. "She's not a *freaking* witch!" It's Josie screaming to the top of her lungs.

"Go back." A voice is whispering to me…in my head. It sounds like Toni. *Really? What's with my legs? They're taking me back.* "Let me through; let me through!" No choice but to push my way into the crowd, jamming my elbow into a few ribs. They're too close to starting a riot.

"Get *off* her!" Josie yells —kicking a girl off Mafdet.

Some dude comes up behind her and is trying to yoke her.

"Watcha think you're doing?" The dude with Wayne rushes in, swinging at his head, slamming his fist into cat's ear.

This isn't good. I didn't come here to fight or to break one up.

But it's too late for any of that now. This mob must think I'm with Mafdet by now anyway; they're making it difficult to get through.

"Is he with them?"

"Maybe he is."

Oh shit.

"Move … move … *move*— get the fuck out the way!" No time to be polite.

A fist is flying at my head, but not quicker than mine at theirs. They're stumbling back. Good, but now two other folks are running at my sides. My hands are springing out reflexively, mushing them in the face. I ain't been in a fight in a while, but my legs are naturally picking up speed, carrying my body—running through them.

Please don't let them find out I'm with DL!

I'm almost over to Mafdet, Wayne's manhandling anyone that comes close. Ray's swinging a chair at others, and Josie's stuck between shielding Mafdet and ramming whatever limb she can into people. Something studded coming towards my nose, again my body is going to into action, ramming my fist into the face of the one who swung it.

Damn, I just hit a woman! I can't get soft-hearted— just push forward to Mafdet. What's this heaviness that dropped onto my shoulders? No one laid a hand on me. Guilt?

I really didn't see her.

Moving towards Mafdet is becoming a fight against my own body. The muscles in my arms, chest and legs keep cramping up. But that weight on my shoulders is different, keeps getting heavier.

"I can't move!"

"What's happening to us?"

"Help!"

"Oh God!"

The desperate screams echoing throughout the auditorium followed by heavy wheezing, whispering out to shortness of breath, doesn't put a battery in my back.

Not one bit.

My stomach is getting queasy—lightning shooting between it and my head. Something else, the smells, people's musk are more pungent…not smelly, but almost the electricity you smell in the air when a storm is approaching.

What's with my chest? It's tightening up…want to just stop and catch my breath. All I can do is clutch at it and wait for it to pass.

If it does.

The question, and a whole mess of others, keeps bouncing around in my head. Two people are charging out for me.

The pain is gone.

"*You!*" It's hard to avoid her accusingly pointing finger.

"You know what is going on, right?" Her voice is struggling to rasp at me.

At least she's open to talk, not fight. I'm tired of fighting.

"Yeah, you're from D.L. I've seen you!" squeezes out the other, who is coming close to choking.

Shit, they can't breathe either…it's not just me.

I can barely talk to tell them to get off my sleeves. *C'mon, stop holding on to me.*

Why did I even let them get close enough so they could pull me down with them while they tremble? They can hardly keep their grips. I can feel their strength leaving their bodies. They collapse.

Good? I mean, they were the only ones who recognized me—glad it doesn't take much to pry their hands from off me.

WTF? Bodies all about me beginning to drop! The deaden thuds of people hitting the floor one after another, jars a lingering suspicion running around in my head. Directive Living *knows more* than what they told me.

Which wasn't much.

I completely forgot about Mafdet, drifting into memories as they string themselves together forming conclusions that I'm not ready to accept.

"AHHHHH!" That unified yell from the ones who are still conscious is right in timing with the lights blacking out. I can barely see what's in front of me now.

It only takes a split second for my daydream to be chased away with what I can make out of the speckled-pattern auditorium floor rushing towards my face. Smashing into the floor is nothing less than like being stabbed through my skull. How couldn't I tell I was near passing out? But I'm happy to even be able to think about it—

Shows I am still alive and conscious.

This throbbing upon throbbing is easing off on spiking, but without it knifing my senses, I can feel my nose … going in two different directions. I wish my face wouldn't slip across the growing puddle of blood when I try to look up. I can't help but to fall right back down after catching a glimpse of the now darkened auditorium.

My eyes are beginning to adjust ... starting to distinguish shapes better. Everybody is passed out.

Well not everybody.

Mafdet is getting to her feet...sluggishly but looking determined to stand.

Why now? Panic is finally settling in. But the crazy thing is I can barely move *to panic*. My throat and lungs are clogging up, the heavy phlegm gathering in them preventing me from breathing properly. Why would my immune system work so hard to try and choke me from the inside? Thoughts racing again—getting weirder. As if all the negative shit I've done in my life is being forced out to the surface ...but wants to stay in.

"Stop cursing." Again, I hear a voice, not my own, speaking in my head ...a voice like Toni's.

Every ounce of energy is moving away from my limbs, pulling—no, draining away from my consciousness and that sensation of something sitting on my shoulders is back; my splitting headache starting to compete with it.

My nose is still leaking, the blood running down my neck; why can't the sensitivity of my senses become weaker like everything else? What's that strange sound getting louder and louder, the sound of liquid filling a large container or huge plastic bag...

Poured from a bucket.

Nothing is making sense anymore. But since all the mess I've gone through this rising, what has made any sense?

Great, right away a separate dizzying tingling is beginning to spin around in my head. Who knows what it is? This is scaring the shit out of me—more than I am already. Why am I struggling to look around, instead of just resting my nearly broken body and waiting for the next thing to happen?

Everyone appears to be surrounded in some type of liquid yolk thing.

WTF? Are those eggs?

I need to stop straining the muscles in my eyes just so I can get more detail on how their bodies are being pushed to curl up in fetal position. Hard to focus—I can just about get their movement, floating and bobbing around in some glowing purplish fluid.

Oh shit, I didn't notice but the same thing is happening to me the whole time. I'm so involved with everyone else I didn't hear the liquid pouring into a membrane swallowed up around me. Can hardly follow my first instinct to bust through it; my limbs are dampened by fatigue. The sound of this strange fluid pouring into my ears and my body slowly rising ...

Is beyond my comprehension.

I want to go apeshit more than ever and claw my way out, but I quickly realize my body has been paralyzed for the last few minutes. All I have are my thoughts ... and they aren't doing shit to help. This gel-like soup has no sympathy for the way it forces itself into all my orifices. It doesn't take long for me to drift and bob about in my own personal egg … like all the others. The temperature of it is so close to my own, it's difficult to tell if I am truly in it.

And breathing. Breathing isn't an issue; my lungs expand and contract like normal. just getting now that I can breathe normally again. A near transparent film slipping over my eyes is instantly blocking out light…even the sparks that come from thinking.

Arrgghh!

The sudden burst of illumination brings back my eyesight. Peering from behind this newly formed film, I can see nothing much has changed in the room, except the varying waves of energy flowing off the eggs. Or maybe I am just able to see what was already there. Limply, but gently revolving in the egg, should have me spazzing out…but peace is taking hold of me.

I can't get any control of my movements, just turning about freely, to face Mafdet…staring at me from the outside. The indigo glow of energy fluctuating out from her eyes is not even surprising at this point, as it illuminates into the egg, crackling out sparks. Her hair, looking woolier than before, standing up, waving about in its own electrical currents.

"Peter Sekham, you don't know what you stumbled into … and you don't know the measure of your importance to it all."

The sound of her voice is unreal, deep but feminine, an airy whisper—but it pushes loudly into the egg and my body.

All I wanted to do was go on vacation.

12am

Made in the USA
Middletown, DE
19 February 2023

24732514R10080